D1103647

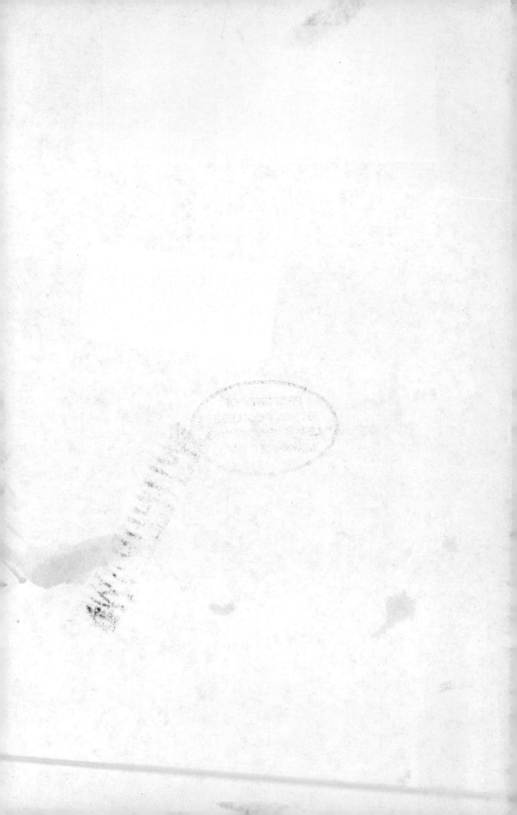

ATONEMENT

ATONEMENT
Gaétan Soucy

A novel

170201

Translated by Sheila Fischman

Published in 1999 by
House of Anansi Press Limited
34 Lesmill Road
Toronto, ON M3B 2T6
Tel. (416) 445-3333
Fax (416) 445-5967
www.anansi.ca

Distributed in Canada by
General Distribution Services Ltd.
325 Humber College Blvd.
Etobicoke, ON M9W 7C3
Tel. (416) 213-1919
Fax (416) 213-1917
Email Customer.Service@genpub.com

Distributed in the United States by
General Distribution Services Inc.
85 River Rock Drive, Suite 202
Buffalo, New York 14207
Toll free 1-800-805-1083
Fax (416) 445-5967
Email Customer.Service@genpub.com

First published in French as *L'Acquittement* by Éditions du Boréal

03 02 01 00 99   1 2 3 4 5

CANADIAN CATALOGUING IN PUBLICATION DATA

Soucy, Gaétan, 1958–
[Acquittement. English]
Atonement

Translation of: L'acquittement.
ISBN 0-88784-641-6
I. Title
PS8587.O913A7213 1999   C843'.54   C99-931351-7
PQ3919.2.S655A7213 1999

Cover design: Bill Douglas @ The Bang
Typesetting: Brian Panhuyzen

Printed and bound in Canada

THE CANADA COUNCIL | LE CONSEIL DES ARTS
FOR THE ARTS | DU CANADA
SINCE 1957 | DEPUIS 1957

*We acknowledge for their financial support of our publishing program the Canada Council for
the Arts, the Ontario Arts Council, and the Government of Canada through the Book Publishing
Industry Development Program (BPIDP). This book was made possible in part through the
Canada Council's Translation Grants Program.*

for Jean

But if memory shows us the past,
how does it show us that it is the past?

— Ludwig Wittgenstein

THE TRAP

THE FUNDAMENTAL DISASTER that fashions the reality of the world is the inevitable death of those we love. And anyone who claims to believe in the unreality of things need only be reminded of the reality of mourning.

Louis was dreaming about when he was a little boy. It was summer: he was standing on the lawn in the garden. He was responding to his father's wave from across the street; he was about to get into his car. His present self, in the booby-trapped body of a forty-four-year-old adult, was standing in the background near a tree, observing the child he'd once been. From inside his dream, he wondered how such a thing was possible. His father was waving again and again, as if those seconds were going round and round in eternity. The little boy was only visible from behind. Could it be that already he no longer had a face?

The feeling of being swallowed drew Louis from his sleep. Not realizing right away where he was, he asked the driver to tell him.

"The road's blocked, Monsieur. We can't go any farther."

"Blocked?"

The vehicle had skidded and sunk into the snow that filled the ditch on the left. And the driver of course was complaining. Still dazzled by his vision of a July morning, Louis had trouble judging the present situation. Was it because he'd dreamed about his father? Everything struck him as peculiar, incomprehensible. Including the strangely affected way the driver grumbled. You'd have thought he was a little boy pretending to lose his temper like a grown-up.

"What will we do?"

"What can we do? We'll go back to the station."

Louis settled himself in his seat with a weary sigh. (Which he regretted immediately: what if the driver thought he was being blamed for something?) For the past eighteen hours he'd done nothing but travel around, cart his luggage, get out of one vehicle and into another, never arriving at his destination. "Is it absolutely impossible? Couldn't we try to free the wheels?"

The driver snorted with a bitter curse. He replied that they'd need at least three horses to get the car out.

"Which means we'll have to go on foot," said Louis, thinking out loud.

"I'm afraid so."

Despite his moaning and groaning, the driver didn't seem overly worried. He'd come into the world in an excellent mood. And the traveller's distracted, at times haggard, appearance couldn't help but stir in him amused surprise. Nothing malicious. His reaction to Louis was like the friendly affection children feel for clowns.

The left side of the car had sunk into the snow in such a way that the door couldn't be opened. With some difficulty, the two men scrambled out the other side. Ahead in the small valley, the road was impassable. Snow had blown into it, forming a vast lake of powder. Louis tightened his scarf around his neck. His only luggage was a small case similar in size and shape to a doctor's black bag. Having wanted to travel light, he had decided at the last minute not to bring his old fur-lined coat, but he realized now that it might have been a mistake. He was wearing just a sheepskin-lined raincoat.

As the driver inspected the vehicle — a Ford from just after the war — Louis gazed at the landscape before him. Already, night was falling. Light seemed to be coming off the snow. In the white dunes the wind had scratched grooves so precise and fine they could have been carved by a craftsman. You could watch them follow the undulating landscape; they were as gentle as the outline of human lips. Here and there a breath of wind stirred up swirls of diamond-like dust that vanished like smoke. A seemingly infinite forest spread out on either side of the valley. The immensity of the landscape, almost violent, charged off in every direction, inflating the space like a balloon.

"No, I think I'll be fine like this," he told the driver, who had suggested snowshoes. (Actually, Louis had never used them and was afraid he'd be clumsy.) He picked up his case. He preferred to carry it himself, because of a reflexive humility and because he wasn't used to being served.

The driver pointed to the expanse of the heavens. "Well, well, would you take a look at that!"

Guilelessly, Louis looked up. The other man laughed softly as he buckled on his snowshoes. The traveller continued to peer at the vault of heaven. The driver grew impatient.

"Ha-ha. It was a joke. There's nothing to see."

"I know." But once Louis's attention had been drawn to the empty sky, it wasn't easy to tear him away.

The train station was two miles distant. The traveller led the way. He felt guilty for having insisted on taking the car and was prepared to cover the cost of towing. He tried to ignore the prattle of the driver, who wasn't much affected by the mishap. Only occasionally did he come out with a couple of crude curses for form's sake, as if he'd suddenly remembered that he was in a foul mood and had to show it. But soon enough he'd resume his carefree humming, life being careful now and then to create individuals with the express function of not bearing grudges.

Louis walked on with his head down, his eyes glued to the whiteness. All he could hear was his own breathing filling the space around his head. By making him relive the last morning he'd seen his father alive (an orphan is a child who ages fifty years at once), Louis's dream had plunged him into such a state that he was still waiting for proof that he was well and truly awake. What was happening now didn't convince him. Perhaps he'd emerged from one dream only to enter another.

What he first took to be a stone suddenly stood up as he approached, and it bristled so abruptly that Louis's shoulders jerked backwards as if from the recoil of a rifle. It was a porcupine, the first one he'd ever seen. "Is it true that you can eat them raw if you're lost in the forest?" He'd once been told that it was forbidden to trap porcupines, that they're reserved for poor wretches lost in the mountains, that their skin, apparently, could be peeled like that of a banana. True or not, the story had marked him and that was why he'd given credence to it. On any subject that didn't touch the essential, you could pull his leg all you wanted. He wouldn't try to correct you, he considered it unimportant. He reckoned he had wisdom enough as far as God, the effects of time, and death were concerned.

The thought of eating an animal raw preoccupied him for over a hundred yards. The snow came up to his calves and it was seeping into his boots. He felt an unpleasant heaviness in his chest. On the blank page he could see nothing but his own stocky shadow and that of his hat, like a half-note rest on a music staff. The driver followed at a consistent distance, as if respecting rank.

Presently they came to the railway track. On the hillside they caught sight of the station lights, which seemed to shine more intensely the closer the men got. It was the effect of the fading daylight, already nearly gone. A few chalets were lit with glimmers so pale that they disappeared if you tried to stare at them, like spots of light when your eyes are closed.

"I beg your pardon?"

"I don't think," repeated the driver, panting, "you'll be able to get to the von Crofts' tonight."

Louis made no reply. In any event he'd never intended to get to the von Crofts' today. But he did want to get to Saint-Aldor, where he'd reserved a room at the hotel. Where would he spend the night otherwise? Would he have to walk the six miles or so between the station and the village?

Louis left the railway track and started along the gravel-covered embankment; he could feel the rough surface through the soles of his boots. He was shivering and at the same time sweating profusely. Fifteen or so men were working along the track, clearing the rails. The driver spoke to them. Louis kept going.

The stationmaster, standing on the platform, didn't take his eyes off them until they'd reached him. He was wearing an overcoat with epaulettes like those you see on navy officers, and the kind of matching cap that turns ladies' heads. With his British moustache, very blond and very fine, and his smoking of a pipe or cigarettes that resembled him (thin, long), he'd opted for Anglo-Saxon composure and its precise, economical movements — a popular look among Canadian NCOs.

A decent fellow nonetheless: around thirty years old, stamped with mental health and military glory, capable of fine angry outbursts. He knew that he was brave, unostentatious, honest by nature (just as others have flat feet or a keen sense of hearing), and he didn't try to take credit for anything more. He accepted his situation stoically, with the calm certainty that his day would come: it couldn't do otherwise in a world where it was enough to do one's duty, where the Allied Forces had finally been victorious, and where a posting to the middle of nowhere wouldn't last forever.

"Out of gas?" he asked as soon as they were close enough that he didn't have to raise his voice.

The driver shook the snow off his snowshoes. "Couldn't drive through the valley."

Louis put his case down and rested his back against the wall. When he had been walking, he hadn't felt tired. Now, though, his body was in distress. His heart was beating as if it were shifting back and forth inside his chest, stars were bursting in tiny explosions on the periphery of his vision. He gazed at his reflection in the window to study the extent of the damage. He saw his stocky silhouette, his fleshy face with full, drooping cheeks — the jowls of a St. Bernard, Françoise would have said, kissing them. Beneath his eyes, shadows created pouches that could have held twenty-five-cent pieces. Unconsciously, he placed behind his ear a lock of black, oily hair in need of a cut. His lips were bluish and swollen like those of a drowned man. Louis turned away, depressed to the point of disgust by his own face.

"Come with me," said the stationmaster courteously. "Come inside and warm up a little. You," he said to the driver, "go fetch the soup from Granny Beaulieu."

Immediately, the driver put his snowshoes back on. They could see him heading for a cabin that gave off a red glow in the distance.

With one hand on Louis's shoulder, the stationmaster ushered him inside.

The heat from a wood stove didn't make Louis feel any better, only more suffocated. He loosened his scarf.

"If you'd like to sit down, I've made tea."

Four armchairs sat in a semicircle before a blazing fireplace. This heat was less aggressive than that from the stove, and, as he made his way to it, Louis finally experienced a sense of well-being. He sat on the edge of his chair so he could bring his numb hands close to the gentle fire.

The officer came back with a teapot that he set down on a small table. He offered Louis a china cup, its elegance contrasting with the lack of refinement elsewhere in the rustic shack. "Here, Monsieur Bapaume. If you don't mind me saying so, that's an odd name, Bapaume. People must ask you to repeat it all the time. But having said that, it's a name I'm very familiar with. It's the name of a county seat in the Pas-de-Calais region and I've been through there, sure as I'm talking to you now."

Louis merely nodded. Generally, unless he was asked a question in proper form, he didn't open his mouth. He was one of those people who, though imaginative and full of resources, feel pressured by the unexciting demands of the moment and are called timid.

The building was barely twenty feet square. In the shadow of the staircase that went to the attic, an orderly stack of ledgers sat on a counter covered with bills, bureaucratic forms, and carefully folded roadmaps. The clock on the central beam showed 5:20 PM. Under it was one of those calendars with a page for every day: December 22.

"Oh, thank you," he said as the officer poured his tea.

Louis had arrived at the station around 2:00 in the afternoon. He hadn't been back to the area for twenty years and, remarkably devoid of a sense of direction (so much so that he inevitably lost his way if he went just three blocks from where he lived), he'd misjudged the extent of the countryside. He'd thought that the village of Saint-Aldor was, in a manner of speaking, right next door to the station, and had assumed he could easily walk there. But the real distance and the heavy snowfall the night before had made that a risky enterprise and the officer advised against it.

The other man's deference kept surprising Louis. His own lack of sparkle, his utter mediocrity in society, his appearance, which he knew he'd neglected — none of it struck him as liable to create any empathy, to say nothing of respect, in an elegant young officer fresh from the Allied victory. All things considered, Louis preferred that no one pay him any particular attention; in fact, he preferred to be treated coolly. He didn't know how to react to kindness. He knew even less that kindness touched him deeply and made him feel a gratitude that verged on anxiety and left him at a loss.

The stationmaster came and sat in one of the armchairs and, with a cordiality that was intended to show his own indifference to social graces, asked: "Now, about Monsieur Bapaume: what sort of work does he do?"

"What sort of work?" Louis murmured, blinking, as if the question had struck him as a strange one that merited some thought. "I'm an organist at Notre Dame Basilica in Montreal. Substitute organist. I . . . Well, I also compose music."

The officer smiled, revealing two gold teeth. "I would have bet. I'd have known at a hundred paces, just by your appearance, that you were a musician."

"Oh yes?"

"My mother is a musician. She taught violin in the old days, when she was still living in Paris."

"How interesting." After such a clumsy response, Louis didn't know how to get the conversation going again. This kind of harmless banter had always been an ordeal for him.

Being obliged to talk, to engage in lighthearted exchanges: dear God! Usually, the other person grasped the situation fairly quickly and didn't insist, leaving Louis to experience bitter relief coupled with a sense of failure and shame.

But the stationmaster could have kept up a conversation with an umbrella. His enforced solitude deep in the countryside, where the village of Saint-Aldor was all there was of civilization, made him itch to pour his heart out, to communicate to a fellow creature something other than orders. He treated Louis Bapaume with the spontaneous complicity of men of the world who find themselves alone together in a crowd of country bumpkins. As happened whenever someone spoke to him, Bapaume was besieged by tics that tightened the muscles in his arms, his thighs, and his back in unpredictable waves, like sheets of heat lightning in a summer sky. And too busy hiding his nervousness beneath a surface calm, he hardly paid attention to what was being said. The soldier was talking about the driver.

"Chouinard is one of those simple souls you just have to dress in a uniform: pin a medal or a little bell on their chest and they'll be overjoyed and filled with such gratitude they'll be devoted to you for life." There was no contempt in his words, barely a hint of affectionate mockery. He could have been talking about a toddler.

"But now that we're obliged to spend the next few hours together, allow me to introduce myself. How ill-mannered of me not to have done so before. Lieutenant Hurtubise. Jacques Hurtubise."

By way of salute Louis rose slightly from his seat. "Delighted to meet you. But I absolutely insist on getting to Saint-Aldor tonight." And, as if this detail subjected him to an urgent duty, he added: "I've reserved a room at the hotel."

Lieutenant Hurtubise winced. "I'm afraid that's impossible. The road won't be plowed till late tomorrow afternoon. At the earliest."

From his experience as a leader of men, the officer had concluded that one must always look them in the eye, which intimidated Louis, who couldn't bear to be looked at. His expression was sombre as he studied the bottom of his cup.

"But you can use my room upstairs, Monsieur Bapaume. I'll sleep down here on a camp cot. Don't worry, it won't be the first time."

"I can't wait till tomorrow evening. I have an appointment with the von Croft family at noon tomorrow. And then I have to be back in Montreal for Christmas. I play the organ at midnight mass." He said this to himself, scowling. He often spoke out loud when he was alone.

"Are the von Crofts friends of yours? Or relatives?"

"No," said Louis. Then, for the first time since the beginning of this conversation, he turned towards the officer. And in a voice suddenly filled with emotion: "Some old business to be settled!" He took a deep breath, like a man who is with great difficulty containing some inner upheaval. But he said nothing more. His eyes were damp. He drained his cup to the last drop, fingers trembling slightly. Hurtubise gazed at him with respect and gravity. Ill at ease, Bapaume set his cup and saucer on the small table.

"Would you like more?"

"No thanks, Lieutenant."

With a contemplative look, the officer made a steeple of his hands, forefingers on his lips. "At the moment I don't see what we can do. Our Jeep has been requisitioned for the corporal, as has our dog team, and neither will be available till the weekend."

The driver came in the back door, which had a spring

and slammed shut with a bang. He held at arm's length in front of him a kettle that gave off a dense white steam.

"Here's Chouinard with the soup."

Chouinard set the kettle on the tiles in front of the wood stove. He had a clumsy walk, a comical waddle like a puppet that doesn't bend at the knees. The room was fragrant with barley, onions, and simmering salt pork. Chouinard joined them and stood next to his officer. "Nothing but wind between his ears," thought Louis admiringly. How old was the man? Twenty-two maybe? He seemed content. He was obeying his lieutenant. Who filled him in on the situation.

Chouinard listened, his head bent towards the lieutenant. Then he turned to Bapaume. "We could ask Maurice."

"Maurice?" Bapaume repeated.

Chouinard spoke to his lieutenant: "The von Croft boy. Of course it's too late tonight. But he could come with the dogs and sled at dawn tomorrow. I know the von Crofts slightly. I could call and ask. They have a phone."

Hurtubise gave Bapaume a questioning look.

"Maurice, you say?"

"Yes, Monsieur Bapaume. Maurice von Croft. A boy of around fifteen."

Louis's jaw dropped. He looked stunned.

"And you think he'd come?" asked Hurtubise.

"I'll phone right away, Lieutenant."

"Call the inn too and tell them the gentleman won't be there tonight. Is that all right, Monsieur Bapaume?"

The prospect of spending the evening with the officer, sharing his meal, submitting to the ordeal of making small talk, perhaps even talking about himself, gave Bapaume the urge to hang himself. For hours he'd been wishing for the anonymity of a hotel room, where he wouldn't have to move, where he could think about nothing but the ordeal awaiting him the next day. But did he have a choice? "I'm very grateful for your hospitality."

"Excellent! Be a good fellow, Chouinard, go and phone. But all this must have given you an appetite, Monsieur Bapaume. We've got cheese, bread, good hot soup. What more can we ask of the Lord?" The officer whistled happily as he set the table. The turn of events had put him in a fine mood. "We're going to talk about music!" he announced brightly.

With an air of constraint Louis replied: "If you wish."

Hurtubise arranged bowls and plates on the table, sliced bread and cut cheese, meticulously, with obvious pleasure. "There we go," he said. "A simple meal, nothing to it!" He began wolfing down bread, cheese, and soup, with no self-control or refinement, as if he wanted to bring out from under his worldly veneer the rough and rather conventional bonhomie associated with a soldier.

Louis joined in, picking at his food as was his habit, pulling off bits of bread as if to feed them to the birds. It wasn't that he didn't eat much. But he spent a long time at it, taking baby steps, so to speak, and one tiny spoonful at a time; still he could easily get to the bottom of a soup-kettle by the end of an evening. It was the same on the rare occasions when he drank.

Chouinard came back.

"The hotel keeper was very understanding, what with the storm . . . but he says they'll want compensation anyway. You understand, they'd cooked a meal . . ."

"I'll pay, they needn't worry. But . . . this young Maurice von Croft?"

The driver became more animated. "He'll be here by noon, not before. On account of the search."

"What search?" asked the lieutenant.

"Apparently the daughter of the Saint-Aldor verger has disappeared. She went off into the mountains first thing this morning. But then it started snowing again. . . . Nobody knows. Now it's too late to continue the search. They'll go out again tomorrow at daybreak."

"We must send some of our men," said the officer, slowly putting down his spoon.

"In that case there's no need for young von Croft to come and get me. I can go with your men."

Hurtubise looked appalled. "That's out of the question! It's a real expedition. They'll be going on snowshoe with packs on their backs! It will be a rough journey — too rough for anyone who isn't used to it. No, no, Monsieur Bapaume, it's best if you wait for the boy."

Louis bowed his head, docile, then went back to his soup, pensive and slow as a bovine. Slipped a bit of cheese into his mouth. His lack of enthusiasm intrigued the lieutenant.

"I hope you're not too disappointed by this modest meal."

Still chewing, Louis waved his hand in protest. "It's just that I'm not a fast eater," he explained after swallowing.

"Take as long as you want."

Louis thanked him. Then, God knows why, a feeling of numbness, of weariness came over him without warning, and all at once eating seemed a tremendous burden. Slowly, he pushed away his plate. "You must excuse me, it's probably fatigue . . ."

"I certainly understand." And to his faithful follower: "Clear this away, if you would."

With a military salute, Chouinard complied straight-away.

Bapaume still had his coat and hat on. Suddenly aware of it, he asked what he should do with them.

"Leave them on the chest till Chouinard brings them up to my room. Your room, that is, for the night."

Bapaume went to the window. Men coming in from the railroad were stowing shovels and machinery in the shed at the end of the platform. He wondered where they'd all sleep. Aside from the shed and the station itself, he hadn't noticed any buildings nearby. Perhaps they'd spend the night in the little cabin the lieutenant had identified as Granny Beaulieu's.

Three of the men had posted themselves on the gallery. They were looking up at the sky and smoking. One had his elbow on the windowsill. Had it not been for the glass, Bapaume could have touched him. The young man was holding his cigarette between thumb and index finger because his other three fingers had been cut off at the knuckle. Catching sight of Bapaume, he modestly moved away from the window, as if he didn't want to be a screen between the traveller and the night.

The moon had risen. So close and so clear that you could count its wrinkles, stick your finger into each of its craters. From Louis's angle, it appeared to be at the summit of an enormous fir tree, like a head of light resting on the tall body of a tree. Or of a bilboquet. Here in the countryside the same brightness prevailed as in a church during a candlelit procession. There wasn't even a breath of wind to stir the snow. Crystals clung to the tips of branches as if by miracle, glittering there, creating so many stars it was as if the Milky Way had taken a wrong turn and had come to rest between the mountains. Why wait then? Why not take advantage of the light and continue the search: you could make out a penny at thirty paces and every minute was precious, wasn't it?

The voice of Hurtubise behind him: "Under the pines you can't see six inches ahead of you."

"But the woman . . . I can't imagine . . . she must know the area? What could have gone wrong?"

"Last summer's rain. There were landslides. In some places it's possible that the mountain landscape looks completely different, even to someone who's known it since childhood. And don't forget, we tend to be less cautious when we feel that we're on familiar ground. An unexpected crevice and you fall thirty yards. Do you know what it's like to fall into a crevice filled with powder snow? The shock may be cushioned, but you still sink in; you sink in as if it were quicksand."

The lieutenant had lit a pipe. He sat there in his armchair, his left ankle on his right knee. "You were saying? Porcupines . . . ?"

"It was nothing, Lieutenant. I was talking to myself. Please excuse me."

On his way back to his chair, Louis stopped at the portrait of a young woman that graced the counter. He had noticed the watercolour earlier that afternoon when he'd arrived at the station. The young woman's name was written at the bottom, and it was the name that had struck him.

"A portrait of my mother as a young girl," the officer had said, smiling. Then he had blushed.

———

Lieutenant Hurtubise spoke on the phone with the people in charge at Saint-Aldor. He wanted some more precise information about the search. Then he went to talk to his men and give them orders for the next day.

Bapaume studied the scores he'd taken out of his case. He

often went back two pages, for he realized that the music was playing in his head by itself and he wasn't paying any attention to it. His chin dropped to his chest and he began to doze off.

The officer laid one hand on his shoulder and he jumped. "Stretch out on the camp cot if you want, till the room is ready."

"No, I'm fine, really. If I sleep now I'll wake up in the middle of the night."

They couldn't hear the commotion of the men on the gallery now, nor the shouts they exchanged from one end of the property to the other.

"But I don't think I'll stay up very late. I have a rough day ahead of me tomorrow."

"Chouinard's gone out to lock the shed. As soon as he comes back he'll prepare the room for you."

"You shouldn't go to so much trouble. I could sleep on the floor, you know."

Hurtubise gazed at Louis Bapaume in silence. He looked as if he wanted to ask a question but didn't dare. A humility close to pleading made the traveller's pupils contract in an odd way, making his eyes very small, like those of a man with a gun to his head. It made Hurtubise feel awkward and, picking up his pipe, he made his way to a corner of the building, where there was a phonograph.

"It's no treasure trove," said the officer, "but I do have a few good recordings. What would you say to some Schumann?"

"That would suit me fine."

Hurtubise handled the records with the jealous (somewhat intolerant and narcissistic) caution of a collector, blowing on the grooves to get rid of the dust. As soon as the first crackling could be heard, he said, "Now tell me, these von Crofts: I don't want to be indiscreet, but who are they?

There can't be all that many Germans around here."

"The *Davidsbündlertänze*," Bapaume murmured when he heard the first bars.

"That's right. You guessed." The lieutenant sat down again. He was waiting for an answer to his question.

Louis shrugged as a sign of ignorance. "I know very little about them. It's been twenty years since I've seen them. I was the music teacher in Saint-Aldor back then. Monsieur von Croft hired me to teach his little girls."

"And you're coming back to see them twenty years later, just like that?"

"It's . . . it's a personal matter."

Again, Hurtubise looked at Louis without a word.

To avoid more questions about why he'd come, Louis began to recount what little he knew about Robert von Croft. He had left Germany in the early 1920s. A cabinet-maker by trade, he'd belonged to a workers' group in his youth and had got into trouble with some extremist circles, God knows how or why. Among other things, he'd married a Jewish woman, which didn't make matters easier for him.

"Obviously," said the officer, with raised eyebrows.

Apparently it was a question of language that, once they'd decided to flee Europe, had prompted them to settle in Canada, for the Jewish woman was of French background.

"That's odd," said Hurtubise, "my mother is Jewish too."

The woman had two daughters, identical twins. And died in childbirth.

"I imagine Monsieur von Croft has remarried since then, because he has a son now. And that's it. That's all I know." Bapaume looked away. With his forefinger he was beating time on the arm of his chair. He felt guilty and vaguely ashamed because Hurtubise had said that his mother was Jewish.

"It will seem odd, I imagine, seeing those people again after so many years. Especially the twins. It's strange. We meet some little girls when they're at the age for nursery rhymes and they're the personification of poetry, on first-name terms with elves and butterflies, whatever you want, and are so appealing they take your breath away. You ask yourself with a kind of giddiness what kind of fairies they'll become when they grow up. And then ten years later you run into them and all they can think about is marrying the notary's son. It's a mystery to me."

"My father was a notary. No one ever came chasing after me to get married."

"That was just my personal impression," said Hurtubise, moving his hand as if to brush away an unpleasant memory.

Bapaume's story had sharpened the curiosity of the officer, who now understood even less about what could have motivated his return after twenty years. With anyone else he'd have overcome his scruples and ventured a straightforward question. But there was something in Louis's attitude — despite his docility and obvious eagerness to comply with the wishes of others — that erected a wall of secrets around him, a wall of weakness that was apt to discourage indiscretions. The record started to skip and Hurtubise got up to turn off the phonograph.

Louis followed the lieutenant out of the corner of his eye. He felt the way he had as a child after he'd performed a Bach Invention and was waiting for the judgement of his teacher, who would also stand at the window, hands crossed behind his back, without saying a word. Louis could have asked the officer what *he* was doing in this neck of the woods. Why was there an armed troop in the midst of these godforsaken mountains? But half from shyness, half from weariness — as well as from resignation to the unanswerable questions that seem to make up the hard core of the world — Bapaume decided not to question the lieutenant.

Who was gazing at the mountains and chewing on his pipe. For a few minutes it was as if each of them had left the other to his business and they were now in separate rooms. Hurtubise took a notebook from his pocket and jotted something in it. Bapaume leafed through his scores. Neither said a word, but within the silence, within the background noise, there was the verger's daughter, who was exercising her power to evoke dread and who came to mind in fits and starts, like the ticking of a clock you suddenly hear.

Chouinard came bursting in, all excited. "Lieutenant! Look what I've got!"

He was brandishing something at arm's length. Bapaume didn't understand immediately what it was. The officer asked Chouinard for the keys to the shed. He handed them over with impatient eagerness.

"But look, Lieutenant, look what I've got! I can't believe it! I'm cording wood. I hear a sound, I look up — and what do I see perched on the post? That's right, a snowy owl! I hit the post with the sledgehammer, just like that, just to bug him, you know how I am. Needless to say it seemed to wake him up. And then he's off into the woods. But look what dropped from his claws!"

"A snowy owl? Are you sure?"

"I swear!"

Chouinard showed off his find under Louis Bapaume's nose. It was a child's toy — a teddy bear. The belly had been ripped open, probably by the bird's beak and claws. It was missing an eye. One of the ears had been torn off. It was probably in the bird's stomach.

"I'll give it to my niece," Chouinard explained. And he took needles and thread from his parka.

This detail amused Bapaume. He wouldn't have been surprised to learn that the parka also contained a hammer, a saw, a frying pan, and a stepladder. For the first time that day, Hurtubise saw the traveller do something that he'd more or less thought him perfectly unable to do. If one could give the name "smile" to the barely perceptible lifting of the corners of his mouth.

Chouinard sat down cross-legged and busily started to mend the teddy bear. A long elastic drop dangled from his nose; he sniffed with serene determination, but it stretched out again, like a yo-yo.

"You can do that later," the officer told him. "Right now I want you to go up and prepare the room for Monsieur Bapaume, who's very tired. And for heaven's sake blow your nose!"

Chouinard did so, on his sleeve. With a hint of sullenness he dropped the toy on the chest, took the traveller's suitcase, and, in three strides, disappeared upstairs.

Hurtubise came out from behind the counter holding a bottle. "This is good local caribou," he said with the appropriate wink. "A little glass or two at bedtime helps chase the nightmares away."

Bapaume wasn't so sure. But his relations with others would have been ten times less complicated if he were a man who knew how to say no. He accepted a drink. At once, Hurtubise started talking about music, because when you buy a drink, you also buy the right to set the topic of conversation. He proved to be what's called an informed music-lover. Where famous recordings and interpretations were concerned, he knew far more than Bapaume, who was no dilettante. Nodding, Louis allowed himself to be taught.

The officer's monologue glided uninterrupted onto the theme of his mother. Louis thought about Françoise. He interrupted Hurtubise in midsentence. He heard himself ask: "Was your father a musician too?"

The officer stuck his thumbnail between his teeth and searched his memory. "Funny, I've never asked myself that question. But I don't remember my mother saying anything about it. You see, I didn't know my father; he died in France when I was eight months old. All I know is, he was a doctor." Hurtubise chuckled innocently for no particular reason. He moved the bottle closer to pour another drop of caribou, but Bapaume put his hand over his glass.

"Thanks all the same, but I don't tolerate alcohol very well. I had a professor of harmony, a nun, Soeur Marie-Ange, who used to tell us: 'Never make the mistake of marrying another musician.'"

Hurtubise, a man who liked to think and refused nothing offered him, weighed the matter. "What about you?" he asked with an eager curiosity that Bapaume found disconcerting. "What do you think about it? Did you marry a musician?" He had noticed the ring Louis wore.

"When I met Françoise she'd just arrived from Paris; she was a violinist in a chamber orchestra."

An incredulous smile on Hurtubise. "No! Really? But what a strange coincidence! My mother's name is Françoise too. It's even written on her portrait over there, behind the counter."

"I'd noticed," said Louis.

The officer seemed delighted by the coincidence.

"The gentleman's room is ready," declared Chouinard as he tore down the stairs. Then he bustled over to the teddy bear as though nothing was more urgent.

The officer turned his attention to the scores that Bapaume had left on a chair. "Are these yours?"

"It's just some music that I've retranscribed," said

Bapaume, closing the notebook and slipping it under his arm. "Now I hope you'll excuse me Lieutenant, but I'm exhausted."

"Certainly, certainly, I've kept you here far too long."

Louis would have preferred to go up without the lieutenant. It was hard for him to relax in a room unless he entered it by himself. (It had taken Françoise a while to get used to the fact that he slept in a cubbyhole near the piano, surrounded by his sheets of music.) That was because the subject of your dreams depends on where you sleep. He hadn't heard that, hadn't read it anywhere; he knew it through the authority conferred by a real-life experience repeated a thousand times. To enter shamelessly into a bedroom, to make noise or to talk with an associate, seemed to him as irresponsible as clicking one's heels in the cage of a big cat that's dozing. One must be careful not to bring on the anger of dreams by rushing them.

"Mind you don't hit your head if you get up during the night," said the officer.

Above the bed, the wall followed the slope of the roof. A small yellow writing desk sat under the dormer window. At the foot of the bed, a rubber tube surmounted a makeshift washbasin into which a trickle of what seemed to be ice-cold water flowed permanently.

"Here's a towel and washcloth. And under the bed you'll find the . . . that is, the . . . chamber pot."

"Thank you for everything."

The officer was taking his time. He went on talking as if nothing had happened. He admitted, turning pink, that he'd tried his hand at the piano — strictly as an amateur, of course, mainly jazz, a field in which Louis's ignorance was absolute and his interest nonexistent. As Hurtubise was about to sit down, Louis couldn't help clicking his tongue impatiently.

"All right then, I'll be on my way," said the officer. Then, with an ingenuous laugh that exposed his gold molars, he said: "It really is amazing. Your wife and my mother. Both violinists, both from Paris — and named Françoise! We could arrange a meeting when I come back, what do you think? My mother lives in Montreal too."

The suggestion, though it was nothing out of the ordinary, seemed to upset the traveller. "I'm not sure," he said. "Or, well, yes, maybe."

Shaking his hand warmly, Hurtubise wished him goodnight, as if all these coincidences were forging an additional tie between them. Bapaume was always surprised by people who are thrilled by coincidences. Who see in them a confirmation that the course of the world has some meaning, that they aren't swimming in a sea of nothingness.

"You could have added that they're both Jewish," he murmured in the direction of the door that the officer had just closed behind him.

He sat for a long moment on the bed. Afraid to lie down, afraid to sleep, afraid to dream, preparing for sleep with anxiety, as if he were getting ready for a fight. It seemed to him that the lieutenant's chitchat had stirred up a dusting of bad dreams in this room, just as an intruder's footsteps can set off a shower of bats in a cave.

He started to undress. He'd been afraid of the cold, for which he had very little tolerance, but as it happened, the chimney passed through the middle of the room and the temperature was, instead, almost excessively hot. He tossed his clothes carelessly onto the writing desk. In the mirror he saw his half-naked body — heavy, hairy, grotesque — and his woeful expression, like that of a big sulky baby. Françoise would have assured him at once: "No, no, you look like Victor Hugo before he grew his beard, everyone says so." He opened his case. From under a pile of scores he took his shaving kit and hunted in vain for the brush. Then, in the pocket of his pyjamas, he found an envelope.

Louis didn't take his eyes off it as he donned his nightclothes. He decided to shave then and there. Even though he thought of all sorts of good reasons not to wait till the following day, he couldn't deny that he was trying to postpone the moment when he'd have to open the envelope. Without his shaving brush, he had to shave dry. In the mirror, the puffy face that looked out at him with sorrow and surprise confirmed his resemblance to Victor Hugo: the Hugo of the early years of exile, the wild-eyed madman of the island of Jersey. While there had been a time when it would have given him a certain puerile satisfaction, today the resemblance was just one more cross for him to bear. It added to the absurdity of his person, like the costumes of kings mockingly given to mental patients in ancient times.

The envelope wasn't sealed. He took out the tooth that was inside. It was a back tooth, his molar for important occasions. It had given him weeks of torture and sleepless nights and three raging toothaches a year before he had decided to pull it himself. That creates ties, and he was attached to that tooth. He would place it on his piano's music stand, like a fetish. When upright, it resembled a standing stone, while on its side you might have thought it was the decapitated head of a dolphin. The root was black, with minute shreds of garnet-coloured mummified flesh. Louis sniffed it cautiously, the way a dog sniffs an old bone, with a reluctant little grimace. Then he shut his eyes and placed it in his mouth. Gently he fitted it into the space where it had lived its life as a molar, then clenched his jaw to drive it in deeper and awaken memories. The exquisite pain made him jump out of his chair. He spat the tooth into his hand. His mouth was filled with the taste of blood.

When he unfolded the sheet of paper, his heart wasn't beating any faster or harder; instead, he had the strange sensation that it was trembling.

My love,
My husband,
My great infinite river,
What is it you hope to accomplish with what you've embarked upon? To suffer? To suffer as though we hadn't suffered enough these last months? To humiliate yourself perhaps? Who do you hope to defeat and what kind of strength do you hope to have proved in the end? An entire lifetime joined me to you, but it seems now as if all that is left is a thread, which shrinks as it's pulled — if you keep moving away from me like this, who knows whether, against all hope, against all expectation, that thread won't break? It is in the name of our love, of what is sacred about it (the events of recent months as well as my own peril ought to make it even more sacred), and in the name of our child that I ask you to give up this absurd plan of yours and to rescue me — I who am a prisoner of the cold, I who am being swallowed up by the everlasting snows.

If it were only the von Crofts! But I know what significance, what gravity you give to all of it, and I believe that you're embarking on a path that has no meaning but your destruction and, at the same time, my own. Who are you to claim that you carry the moral order of the world, its stability, on your shoulders? Oh, I know, you'll tell me that it's not just you, that you're only obeying the demands of your duty — which, in fact, you've exaggerated all your life. But you forget that I'm there too, I who exist only through you, I who would be swept away with you in your fall should you persist in wanting, on your own, through your own initiative, to hurl yourself into the void. And when it's all over, my love, how will the face of the universe have been changed?

Yes, come back to me . . . But come back to your own work too, Louis, to your work! I reread the letter from Olivier Messiaen. Do you truly understand what it represents, what a fraternal gesture it is, what encouragement to persevere? I can't find the words to tell you how desperate I felt the morning when you came to my room, looking distraught, as if you hadn't slept all night. And I know — oh, don't lie to me! — I know that you'd been drinking. I'll never forget your eyes (which were avoiding me, shunning me) when you said: "I've abandoned my oratorio." Yet surely you were not unaware that for months, I owed my life to that music? Have you forgotten that it was a matter of nothing more and nothing less than saving me? Have you forgotten your promise? I'll leave it to others to laugh about it, but if my truth is strange, it's still my truth, and I declare that I need that music to exist. Can you understand that? Not merely to give meaning to my life. But to breathe, Louis, just to breathe.

I shall commit the sacrilege of declaring that I know where God stands on the matter. He joins with me to order you — No! not to order you, for we have to believe, despite the terrible thing that has happened to us, that God does not use violence — to beg you, yes, beg you not to commit the CRIME of not completing that work. Come back, my love, I implore you. Forget about all the von Crofts of this world if there's still time. I will love you no matter what happens. But hurry. My fingers are frozen. There's hoarfrost on the windows. I can barely feel my heart beat in my chest.

Your wife before God,
Françoise

Louis switched off the lamp. He'd been leafing through a photo album published by the armed forces, which the lieutenant had left in the room. He was sitting now on the blotter on top of the writing desk, looking out at the night one last time before getting into bed. Tears flowed by themselves, quietly, with no sobs. He wasn't the one who was crying. Louis still allowed a part of himself, a part that had become foreign to him, to shed any excess tears. But he no longer recognized that he himself had that right. His heart was swollen with shame. He had proven himself completely unworthy of life.

Clouds invaded the sky with fascinating speed, as in a horror film. Soon a grey stupor was all that could be seen of the snow, and the countryside had faded into the darkness. There was only a ring of the firmament on the horizon, blue like a bruise, where one last star was shining like a splinter of mirror in the sun. Louis was thinking about the verger's daughter. What was she feeling now, if she was still of this world? When she began to despair of being rescued, perhaps she saw the sky closing above her and felt like a fly imprisoned by the growing shadow of a spider, and saw that feverish star burning with the intensity of something that doesn't want to die and resembling an appalling, silent cry.

Louis drew the curtain and laid his head on the pillow. The star was still visible through the lace curtain. He closed his eyes and it seemed as if he could still see that star; he thought about the young princess in the legend who cannot erase the bloodstains from her hand.

Anonymous presences spread as slowly as smoke in the shadows around Louis, along with a sensation of gentle touching, of whispering in his ear. His shoulders grew numb. He made awkward movements, as if to keep his head out of water. Freed from clocks, time fell apart. Louis suddenly realized that he was giving the verger's daughter the features of Françoise, but it was too late. With the stony weight of sleep around his neck, he sank straight down into the eddy of dream.

The crack of a whip made Louis sit up in his bed and bump his head on the sloping ceiling. There followed a clattering shudder evocative of castanets. And then nothing. It seemed to have come from under the writing desk. With his mind still hazy, he lit the lamp and bent down.

A mouse was in the midst of expiring, its neck caught in a trap. One paw was still jerking spasmodically. Louis grabbed the creature by its tail.

He muttered incoherently as he extricated the mouse; blood dripped onto his bare toes; he moved like a sleepwalker. He threw the animal into a dark corner of the room. Under the trickle of water, his eyes closed, he scrubbed the trap vigorously to get rid of any spatters, then shook it dry. Finally, before returning to the confusion of his dream, feeling as if he'd accomplished a duty, he tossed it casually into his suitcase.

THE BEAUTY SPOT

HE WAS WAKENED by the howling of the dogs. He looked at his watch. It was after 10:00. Could the von Croft boy be there already? Why had they let him sleep so late?

The sun was coming in through the dormer window, a sword thrust into the half-light. Louis tried to glance outside but the light was so bright that he shrank back as if he'd been slapped. There was a knock at the door. He pulled on his trousers. The lieutenant was standing there in shirtsleeves.

"I couldn't wake you. I was afraid you were sick. You were dreaming, talking about porcupines. How do you feel this morning?"

"I don't know yet."

"The von Croft boy is here."

"Maurice? . . . Ask him to wait. Just give me a minute to wash up." Louis shut the door and stood with his hand on the door frame. The pounding of his heart reverberated in his ears, throbbed in his wrists. He was overcome by nerves.

On his way down the stairs he spied Maurice von Croft sitting in front of the fire. The boy was wearing a heavy coat that made his shoulders appear broad. His tow-coloured hair was plastered to his temples, as if he'd been sweating under a hat. An inexplicable emotion gripped Bapaume. "Yet I have nothing to do with him," he thought. "*He's* not the one I have dealings with."

The boy stood up as Louis approached. He had sharp features with small brown eyes that were nervous and shifty. He barely murmured "good day." He seemed anxious to carry out his orders. He donned a leather cap lined with fox fur, the earflaps pulled down over his cheeks. Outside, dogs were barking.

"Will you look at that imbecile," laughed Hurtubise. He was gazing out the window at Chouinard, who was having fun provoking the animals, mugging and gesticulating.

A card table had been set up by the fireplace. A checkered cloth, cretons, a round loaf, barley soup, jam, and homemade butter. Hurtubise had seen to everything, no doubt including some details that his guest hadn't noticed. The aroma from a steaming coffee pot blended with that of the cedar logs hissing in the fire. There was no question of turning down a meal prepared with such amiable care, and Bapaume resigned himself to it. Young von Croft, who was shy and hesitant, eventually accepted the lieutenant's invitation. He eagerly took the jar of jam and spread some on his bread.

"No news yet," the officer replied to Bapaume's question. "They're continuing the search."

Hurtubise had the drawn features of a man who has slept badly. He joined them around the table but, declaring that he'd already eaten, smoked a cigarette. Bapaume guessed that he was preoccupied by the verger's daughter (out of compassion, of course, but also perhaps because he'd sent some of his men and the reputation of his troop — and his own honour as their leader — was at stake). Louis chewed away without appetite, trying to think about something else so as not to give in to the disgust that food provoked in him in the morning. The windows were so spattered with light, you could see hardly anything through them.

The teddy bear found the day before had been mended and now sat in a prominent position on the counter, its head leaning against the telephone. Chouinard had sewn on a trouser button to replace the right eye, but one ear was still missing. Louis couldn't take his eyes off it. Maurice von

Croft had smeared jam all around his mouth as he ate. No one was saying anything. Hurtubise was absentmindedly smoothing a corner of the tablecloth.

Louis got up from the table.

"Don't forget, the last train leaves at 8:00 tonight."

"I think I can be back long before that."

Maurice immediately went to the door, followed by the lieutenant.

"I'll be right with you," said Bapaume as he went up to the room to get his bag.

The dogs, Samoyeds, shook themselves as soon as they saw young von Croft. They rubbed against each other, exchanged nips, sniffed the ground or their neighbour's rear end, as colleagues are wont to do. Chouinard was lugging some cases along the platform. His silhouette stood out, black against the blazing blue sky. There were no clouds. The glare off the snow was so bright it was as painful as poking a finger in your eye.

Maurice plunged his hand into a bucket of coal and drew a broad black line across his cheekbones. The officer advised Bapaume to do the same. Louis complied, but couldn't see much difference; the light was still just as blinding. His legs were like jelly, the dogs filling him with a childish fear. He walked in a semicircle to avoid going near them. He took his seat in the sled. The officer spread a blanket over his legs.

The team consisted of a dozen animals. Maurice von Croft settled Louis's case against his shins. "You aren't too uncomfortable?"

The gentleness of the voice, which he was hearing now for the first time, the richness of its timbre, struck Louis as so unusual that he asked him to repeat what he'd said, so he could hear it again. But the boy only stared at him.

"I'll be fine I think," said Louis.

Maurice got up on the back of the sled.

"Don't forget, Monsieur Bapaume! Eight o'clock! In any case, I'll be expecting you!"

The dogs took off instantly, like starving creatures chasing a quarter of bloody meat held before them. Chouinard caught up to them with much shouting. He ran full tilt alongside the sled till he could no longer keep up with it.

"Don't forget to bring me some postcards of Saint-Aldor!" he shouted, his hands cupped around his mouth. Then, he picked up handfuls of snow and began tossing them into the air. The crystals shimmered against the blue sky as they fell and Chouinard admired them so much it made him laugh. That was what Lieutenant Hurtubise had meant when he said that the guy had the right sense of values.

The sled arrived at the small valley and, after driving around it, began to travel along the edge of the forest. The road here was a thin ribbon, not wide enough for an automobile. Maurice had to constantly use the handlebar to steer the dogs back on the road when they threatened to spill over it. They were travelling at top speed. Low branches lashed the sides of the sled, grazing the dogs, though without slowing them. Louis felt as if he were falling. The air made his ears ring. The cold, as scalding as the blast from a forge, stung his cheeks. Light burst from all around; it was as deafening as screams.

A pistol shot rang out across the countryside and the strips of snow that streaked the edge of the small valley cracked, crumbled, collapsed in entire sections at a time.

"Who's that shooting? Won't it endanger the search if there's an avalanche?"

"Don't ask me."

Inside the woods, the team drove onto an even narrower road. Maurice slowed the animals. Snow fell from the branches either in light squalls or in dense clumps as heavy as sacks of flour. Louis pulled the blanket over his head. The Samoyeds' panting saturated the air with mist. You could inhale the powerful odour of their breath.

The boy didn't say a word. But now that the pace was slower, he ventured a hesitant glance Bapaume would have liked to have held with a word or a gesture, but the boy's eyes looked away as soon as they met his gaze. They were two shy children who get along well from a distance on the playground but dare not make the first sign of recognition. Louis found himself almost wishing for a mishap: that they'd lose their way, for instance, or that the sled would land in a ditch. He wanted to share something with the boy, even trouble.

The closer he came to his destination, the more his trip lost its urgency. He wished he could take a brief holiday from himself, a burst of complicity before the ordeal.

There was a Thermos wedged in the bottom of the sled. Louis assumed that it was full of hot coffee. To sip some while he sat in the shadow of a rock, thinking of nothing, together and alone in the midst of the snow, covered by the same blanket, surrounded by a silence that would be like the music of this whiteness — it wouldn't have been a crime. He could even — who knows? — take Maurice's hand in his . . .

As if Bapaume's wish was being granted, the boy stopped the team in the middle of a clearing. He walked to the edge of the woods, spread his legs. "Turn around!" he shouted over his shoulder.

Louis blushed. He heard a drumming as the hot liquid pierced the icy crust.

Another detonation shook the crowns of the trees, sending down more heavy loads of snow. Louis turned in Maurice's direction. He saw a yellowish trace in the snow, still steaming, but the boy had gone. Bapaume stood up, looked around him. He wanted to call out but Maurice's name was stuck in his throat; he felt incapable of shouting it.

The team took off by itself and Louis nearly fell out of the sled. His hand groped for the brake. He spied young von Croft in the middle of the road, and the boy, with one bold leap, climbed onto the runners of the speeding sled.

"I was frightened," said Bapaume with his hand on his heart.

The boy didn't reply.

The path led out of the woods and, in the shadow of the mountain, Louis saw the Saint-Aldor-de-la-Crucifixion School.

It was there that on his return from Europe after two years of massive, obsessive studies, he'd come to work, driven by the keenest sense of a mission to be accomplished. Because this orphanage standing alone deep in the forest seemed to him to shelter the world's most destitute, it had attracted him like a promised land. During his twenty-two months of misery in Paris, tormented by his teachers' demands and by his constant worries about money, he'd nonetheless found a way to fill his head with all kinds of incongruities: a muddle of bodybuilding, homeopathy, vegetarianism, nudism, Far Eastern religions; he'd even hung out with some long-haired young people who hovered around the Surrealists. And at night, with his brain on fire, he'd worked at devising a "natural" method for teaching music.

Which he then brought home with him, longing to try it out, convinced that it would be successful when put to the test. At the time he'd honestly thought he could teach anyone, including philistines or boors, the mysteries of the tonal system, the harmonic keys, even atonality — the discovery of which while in Europe had been like a revelation to him. He'd often repeated to Françoise that had his enterprise been successful, he'd have been a different man.

A saint perhaps. He had the necessary qualifications, as he possessed not an ounce of conceit and had always been careful to lock his boundless pride within himself. But in no time at all things turned to disaster and he'd left Saint-Aldor after a year, booed, disparaged, hated, humiliated by a shower of snowballs (some of his colleagues had even taken part in that parody of a stoning). Over the years, just hearing the name of the town would make him leave a room; he'd feel hot under his skin and experience a mixture of unbearable apprehension and shame, like the panic in your own presence that you feel on the day after getting blind drunk, when you realize you've made a fool of yourself.

When he'd finally decided to go back to the village after twenty years, it was with surprise, and a touch of relief for which he still wouldn't forgive himself, that he'd learned that the buildings were now occupied by the Brothers of the Christian Schools. The orphanage no longer existed.

They drove around the steep slope of Mount Saint-Aldor. The dogs, winded now, had slowed down. The breeze played gently in their ruffled fur. They shuddered as they greedily gulped the air. Their flanks heaved, doubling in volume.

The team drove across farmland. Smoke rose like a prayer from the chimneys of log cabins in the distance. Bapaume felt as if he'd never seen them before. The profiles of the mountains, the twists and turns of the frozen river, the woods and solitary rocks that lined the fjord and that, through the enigmatic silence of their forms, evoked the debris of a bygone religion: none of them spoke to his memory. There was a final climb up a gentle slope. Then the first houses appeared, dominated by a church steeple which Louis recognized immediately, in the way you recognize a beloved face.

The dogs, on familiar territory now, made their way without guidance. The village was depopulated. Or at least no one was on the main street. Bapaume reminded himself that the men were no doubt taking part in the search for the verger's daughter. But where were the children? The school, half-hidden by the church, seemed empty when they drove past it.

The team came to a halt in front of the general store without Maurice's having to lift a finger. Habit could explain it. But Bapaume shivered to his very bones.

"I'll be right back." The boy leaped out of the sled and strolled nonchalantly into the store.

The dogs lay flat on their bellies. With their muzzles on their paws, they were trying to get their breath back. Louis envied their quiet awareness, even the expression in their eyes, the striking intelligence, the gentleness too, that was so unlike the ferocity he'd attributed to dogs since childhood.

Bapaume was wrapped in his blanket. He had the impression that curtains were being drawn aside, that faces were pressed against windows, spying on him. Now and then, smothered by the cold air, he heard . . . yes, they sounded like moans of pain. He imagined Françoise's moans during her labour. These sounded the same.

To disguise his discomfort, he pretended to take an interest in the church. It was built of fieldstone, with a blue roof and a tin steeple. It was so familiar he felt it was smiling at him. His immediate surroundings too. The rest — the houses, the general store, what seemed to him to be a hotel, even the street — all were as foreign to him as on the first morning.

As was the von Croft house. Though he delved into his memories, his recollection remained foggy and nothing occurred to him. Perhaps it was right before his eyes and he didn't know it. How could he have forgotten so much in this village where he'd spent thirteen months of his life?

The bell above the store door tinkled. It wasn't Maurice. A long silhouette, thin and sad, emerged onto the steps. It wore a grey, knee-length coat. The collar and cuffs were of the same fur as the hat. The woman might have been in her mid-forties. Her outfit, which suggested a concern for elegance but in the style of fifteen years ago, her gaze, in which a remnant of desperate youth had survived, and something elusive about her bearing, something ridiculous yet touching, all made you suspect that she was a woman on her own, a woman whose heart hadn't been used very much, who (to crown her bad luck) seemed intelligent too. The mere sight of her suggested, who knows why, that her well-ordered life concealed a shocking secret. She took only an absent-minded glance at the sled. But she did slow down, gazing at the traveller again. Then stopped.

"Who is that? She seems to recognize me."

Maurice von Croft came out of the store with a parcel under his arm. The team started up, again without the slightest signal from the boy. Louis continued to look at the woman. She was watching the sled move away, her arms at her sides, stunned by surprise.

The von Croft house stood at the other end of the village. Excitement close to joy took hold of Louis. The curved wings of the roof, the red stone, the windows standing on dripstones and Victorian mouldings: all of it, from his very first glance in more than twenty years, became familiar again.

"We're here," said Maurice.

"I know." Then, as if excited by this unexpected memory, he added proudly: "That's new!" He pointed to a wooden shed covered with shingles that was adjacent to the rear of the house.

"I don't know. It's always been there."

"You're too young. It wasn't there twenty years ago."

Maurice merely shrugged. Bapaume had spontaneously ventured a personal remark and wondered if he'd made a gaffe.

They were about thirty yards from the house. Was it because he was standing on his father's land that Maurice no longer had the look of a frightened weasel, a look that Bapaume had observed at the station?

Maurice got out of the sled and stood waiting in the snow. "I have to go help with the search."

Louis hadn't considered the possibility that the boy might not be with him at the moment of his ordeal. He didn't know exactly what he expected of him, but suddenly the prospect of not feeling Maurice's presence at his side frightened him. The boy was waiting obediently. Bapaume hoped for a sign of friendship, the beginning of a smile, even if it were just in the eyes, but there was nothing; the boy's face remained impassive. Maurice took his hand out of his mitt to brush away a lock of hair that was tickling his cheek. A slender, powerful hand with prominent lines, admirably lithe — the noble hand of a pianist. Louis didn't dare smile. Whenever he caught a glimpse of himself in a mirror, he thought that his smile made him look simple-minded. Reluctantly, he stepped out of the sled and his legs, asleep for the past three-quarters of an hour, buckled under his weight and made him grimace.

Immediately the boy grabbed hold of the handlebar. Wrapped in the fog produced by the dogs' breathing, he headed for the mountain without a word. One rescue team was coming back. They formed black spots in the blazing whiteness, and from this distance they could have been flies that had alighted upon a mound of sugar.

"Like seeing a person you'd assumed was dead reappear," he thought, picking up his case. He was thinking about the astonishment on the face of the woman outside the general store.

———

It was Robert von Croft who opened the door. The man had seen him through the transom, and Louis hadn't even had to ring the bell. He was a tall old man, bony and robust. Images of an easel or a stepladder popped into your head at the sight of him. His crippled left foot was encased in a leather shoe that resembled a horse's hoof. Despite his wrinkles he still had an impassive face from which few of his thoughts could be discerned and piercing eyes that were cautious and sly and that flashed from deep within their sockets. Nor had he shed his German accent, and it was in a worn and rasping voice that he said: "You should have waited till next year when the railway comes and you can travel by train. The work is supposed to begin in the spring. You had no trouble with Maurice?"

"Umm, no," said Louis, who didn't know what to make of this question.

"He's a rascal," said von Croft. And with a bow from another age, another world, he invited Bapaume to come in.

The moment he stepped inside the house, Louis spied the young woman. In his letter of reply, old von Croft had given Louis a simple way to tell the twins apart: Julia had developed a beauty spot above her lip, that she hadn't had as a child. Which meant that the young woman standing in front of Louis was Geneviève. She made the beginning of a curtsy, ostentatiously casual. Bapaume stood there unmoving for a moment, astonished to see in this mature woman the features of the little girl. Geneviève met his gaze without flinching, with a hard smile that contained defiance. She was around thirty. Features pleasant, no more than that, but with a vivacity and a hint of shyness in the eyes, something subtly unsettled, suited to daydreamers brought up in remote solitude, and capable of cataclysmic passions. Bapaume timidly offered her his hand, which she ignored.

"Take off your coat for heaven's sake!" she snapped. And helped him do so and then, with her head held high, took his coat away into another room.

"That's it," he thought. "She's still angry with me."

He followed Robert von Croft into the dining room, where they seated themselves at opposite ends of the table. Louis leaned his elbows on it, with his knees apart and head down. For weeks he'd been imagining this scene. Day by day he had gathered a little courage to face it, knowing he wasn't particularly intrepid and counting on his daily efforts, the way a poor man saves money, penny by penny. And now, just when he could have used it, he lacked the nerve and none of the practice had made any difference.

But he was irritated by his weakness and, prompted by an unvoiced urge to be rude, he took the plunge. "I've come here to talk to Julia."

Von Croft raised his eyebrows. "About what? Julia's already married!"

This remark, which fell within preoccupations unrelated to his own, left Bapaume flabbergasted. "But that's not the reason. I . . . I have to talk to her. A personal matter. An important one for me. For her too perhaps."

Geneviève arrived, her hands full of dishes. She plunked them down hard, obviously intending to make a noise. "In that case, cher Monsieur, your visit is pointless. My sister won't be here today."

"But I'd asked her in my letter . . ."

"I can't help that," she said with a hint of suppressed irritation. "Julia hasn't lived here since her marriage. Maurice is at boarding school and only my father and I still live in this house."

"Is Maurice's mother dead then?" Bapaume wondered.

Geneviève arranged on the tablecloth a plate of fritters, two bottles of pale cider, and some galettes still warm from the oven and exuding an aroma of cinnamon and apple.

"Don't worry, Monsieur Bapaume," said von Croft, uncorking a bottle and offering it to him. "Julia may come back at any moment. She's a midwife, I don't know if you were aware of that. Someone came for her in the middle of the night. A woman in labour. It must be over by now." He started to laugh. "The poor mother is flat-chested: it will make for a resourceful child."

Louis remembered the moaning he'd heard on his way through the village. So he'd been right. Had that been it? An obstacle loomed into his mind, one that could complicate the execution of his plan. "Her husband . . . ?"

Von Croft raised a hand as broad as a bear's paw. "Oh, that one's always gallivanting all over the country! He's gone to town. We expect him back for New Year's Day."

Von Croft was about to add something, but he was overcome by a coughing fit. He coughed like a motor that can't start, and turned red. In a burst of solicitude, Bapaume moved towards him, but the old man gestured to him not to. Finally it eased off. With his eyes closed, von Croft sucked on the result of his efforts for a few moments. Then, concealing himself behind his shoulder, he expelled it into a handkerchief the size of a pillowcase.

"Help yourself," he said, pointing to the dishes. He himself tucked into an apple galette. His teeth were so wobbly that he had to straighten them with his fingers after every bite. He took a long swig from his bottle of cider. From the kitchen, Geneviève displayed her mood by slamming cupboard doors and shoving chairs. Von Croft offered a good-natured expression, as if to say, don't mind her, that's the way she is.

Bapaume took a biscuit so it would look as if he had a reason for being there. The decor in the dining room and living room had changed. In Louis's memory there was an impression of austerity and sobriety verging on the lugubrious. But since his day, young girls had come through like a whirlwind and the walls had been painted the colours of fruits; there were music boxes, crocheted doilies, cozy armchairs, knickknacks as fragile as the fingers of little old ladies. Through the flounces and frills, fine dust particles danced in the sunbeams, giving off sparks as delicate as fairies' sighs. Louis tried to locate the piano. He remembered that it was in the living room on the other side of the door curtain.

On the buffet, between bookends shaped like the heads of wolves, stood a Bible and some school books. A Latin textbook too, open and lying facedown, as if someone had just been reading it.

"Is your son a student?"

With his mouth still full, von Croft chuckled sardonically. "He's in boarding school nearby, with the Christian Brothers. He's come here to spend the holidays with us. Pay no attention to him. He's a rascal." With his tongue, the old man removed some crumbs from his gums. He kept chuckling, his eyes sparkling, his expression merry, as if he were enjoying a good joke or remembering some youthful escapades.

Geneviève reappeared abruptly at the first opportunity, like a vaudeville character champing at the bit in the next room. "Time for your nap, Papa! My father's an old man, you mustn't tire him."

"I'll come back later," said Louis, getting to his feet.

The old man protested that it was too cold and that, in any case, there was nowhere to go in the village. "Even the church is closed! No, please oblige me, Monsieur Bapaume. I've asked my daughter to fix up the living room for you. You won't be disturbed there. There's the big sofa if you'd like to rest. In any case, I won't sleep more than an hour. Make yourself at home! Play the piano if you want, it won't disturb us, as long as my rascal hasn't put it too out of tune."

Louis, who had bent down to pick up his case, was startled. "Is he musical?"

Von Croft chuckled again, shrugging. "Don't make me laugh!" The old man started up the stairs, holding on to the banister. His shoe made a rapping sound like the three knocks in a French theatre that signal when the show is about to begin.

Geneviève showed Louis to the living room. Her airs, her manners, her intonations all showed that she was just obeying orders, that if it were up to her . . .

The annotated scores piled up on the piano brought Bapaume to a halt.

"My brother sings in his school choir," she explained

curtly. "But I don't know what he'd think about you going through his music."

He pulled his hand away as if he'd just touched something blazing hot.

"I'll leave you now, I've got things to do."

Louis collapsed onto the piano bench. He was alone now for the first time that day, and for a man like him, so hungry for solitude, it was as if he'd just spent three sleepless nights. The room was cool, darkened by heavy curtains. After the riot of brightness, it was a relief. He approached the scores with their pencilled annotations. A song for choir a cappella, in counterpoint, in the baroque style. He studied the three pages spread open on the music stand. As he read, as he discovered the intelligence and serenity of the perspective, his heart beat faster. He glanced behind him, afraid of perhaps being taken by surprise, then he picked up the sheets and read the pages that followed. Who could have composed it? It took Louis's breath away. He leafed through the scores and angrily opened the books, like a burglar slashing pillows in search of the family jewels. But there was nothing to be done, the music broke off abruptly after seven pages.

Louis looked straight ahead of him, stunned. So this was what young Maurice was devoting himself to! He started reading again, unable to believe his heart. The retranscription itself, the music signs, had been put down with geometric clarity by a steady, seasoned hand, and the result had the sparkling quality of a Mozart manuscript. And the keen, intelligent annotations betrayed a genuine understanding of this marvel of counterpoint! Bapaume suddenly felt light-headed and had to rest his head on his hands.

He struck a chord in the low notes and pressed his forehead against the resonance chamber until the sound had died. A terrible hope swelled his chest, terrible because of its beauty, and Louis was afraid of giving in to it. Was it possible that Maurice had composed this piece? Unsteadily, he went to the window and lifted the curtains. No sign of young von Croft.

Louis felt cheated, at loose ends, and full of self-mockery. He picked up some knitting that lay on the easy chair and placed it on his head in a parody of an eighteenth-century wig. He gazed at his reflection in the little mirror above the piano. "Johann Sebastian Bach," he thought, snickering to himself. He made a face at his reflection. Then, in a movement full of suppressed frustration, he threw off the knitting.

Françoise, Françoise,
My darling, my love,
My barefoot princess,
How I miss you, you and our child! It seems that in wartime, the poor soldiers who have suffered an amputation continue to experience pain in their missing leg. It's called a phantom limb. And you who talk to me about God in·your last letter! . . . Your last letter that you hid in my suitcase as if you couldn't talk to me. But as you know very well, I've been cut off from God for months now! I experience a kind of PHYSICAL inability to believe in Him. Oh, I know what you'll say: "Jesus, Buddha, Supreme Being — call it whatever name you want!" If it were just a simple matter of words! I only exist through my conviction that I know better than God what our duty is — my own, anyway. As long as we believe in Him, we act according to His law, hoping secretly to please Him. It's as if we were swaying our hips before God, trying to seduce Him. We can only measure the true requirement of duty if we lose all hope of receiving anything from Him. I am now at that point.
I also wish that you'd stop reminding me constantly about

my oratorio, I beg you. I'm being punished, Françoise, can't you understand that? I'm being punished for my pride. I know, alas, that henceforth I'll never be able to invent music. The delicate thread that joined me to Grandeur has been cut by I know not what scythe. Now I feel bare-headed. I feel cold up above, the way your hands feel cold when you've lost your gloves.

He broke off his writing, kept from pursuing it by the presence of Geneviève. A narrow door connected the living room to the scullery and it was to a narrow table there that Geneviève had come to peel her potatoes, as if she wanted to keep him under surveillance. Her stiff movements betrayed the same suppressed anger as earlier. She gave him sour, nasty smiles.

"You're angry with me, aren't you?"

She asked him to say it again, he'd spoken so faintly. "Me? Why should I be angry with you, Monsieur Bapaume? You haven't done anything to me." And she looked him squarely in the eyes, her gaze like a slap.

Yes, Françoise, I am devastated. And your own sadness, your despair, overwhelms me. Every morning I open my eyes with the hope, which is growing weaker by the day, that you will have regained even the slightest appetite for life. I come up to your bed, your head is resting on the pillow, burning hot, and your body chills me. Your hair is pulled back off your face and I hold you close. But then I see your red eyes, your face ravaged by fatigue, and I realize that you've spent the night crying and I feel my entire soul drained of its substance. We can do nothing, of course, about the terrible situation we've been placed in, and I don't reproach you for not fighting. But you've given me the painful obligation of having to fight for two. You have relied on me too much. I try with all my might to go back up the steep

Gaétan Soucy

slope, scraping my hands and knees on the rough edges of the rock while your body, naked, inert, as icy as remorse, is joined to me by a cord that cuts into my waist, that is pulling me towards the abyss of your grief.

You care about life only because of my music, you told me, and I believed you — dear God, how I believed you! I threw myself into that oratorio with a pride verging on delirium. Ah, that fine promise! It was going to save us, no less, justify us before God and man, cleanse us of our material woes, transform our poverty! . . . But at the end of it all I understood, with a certainty that brooked no argument, that this Magnificat, as you called it, reflected no grandeur, only the extent of my own presumptuousness. I, in turn, feel cut off from any source, from any life; it's horrifying to measure the extent of my dereliction. How could I have been so wrong about that bombastic music, how could I have been mistaken for so long about its worth? I was fired by inspiration, touched by the forefinger of Yahweh, seething with creative will, but I was nothing but a sick man, a poor lunatic who can't see the pathetic results of his agitation. I resembled those old women who paint their cheeks, don blonde wigs, put on airs, deck themselves out as if they were twenty, and think in their pathetic madness that the stunned looks turned in their direction are filled with admiration.

Forgive me for having shattered like an egg under the weight of this task. Forgive me for having all the flaws of a talented man, without the talent!

And you, my poor Françoise, you've been a party to this folly. Oh, quite unwittingly. I should have seen that pain had made you distraught too. But how can I make you understand that without wounding you even more deeply, without questioning the clarity of your musical judgement, which is so sound? If it should come about, through some unimaginable grace, some unhoped-for return of pity and justice, if it should happen, yes, that I hear within myself again the slightest call, the slightest chord, the slightest note that shows me, like a sign from on high, that I can, that I must continue to write music, I swear I'll respond to it. Ah! believe me, I WILL FALL TO MY KNEES, MY ARMS OUTSTRETCHED AND MY FACE RAISED UP TO HEAVEN!

But I doubt such a thing is still possible. I don't say that out of indifference. On the contrary, the mere thought of no longer composing, the prospect of an entire life cut off from creative hope, makes me feel the same dread I'd experience if I were to wake up after being buried by mistake, shut inside a coffin. If I still have the slightest chance of salvation, it lies in what I've come to do in Saint-Aldor. In fact, I have no idea where the acts I'm preparing to commit will lead. What I find here may not be what I've come in search of. Perhaps I'll find something I didn't know I was looking for. What does it matter? This is my last chance. If it destroys me, as you say, that's too bad — or rather, so much the better! There's a limit beyond which a man must not be required to burden the earth.

From the distance came the sound of panting and the jangling of bells and chains. The same question could be seen in his eyes and hers. Geneviève got up and disappeared in the direction of the dining room. Young von Croft was on his way home with his dogs.

———

Louis stayed in the living room as if he were being held prisoner there. If he shifted the door curtain he could see Maurice sitting at the table, slowly leafing through his Latin textbook. He could have been the subject of a painting. All the darkness in the world, the ignorance, the solitude, the poverty, was redeemed by that spark of light: a child bent over a book. *The Orphan and His Mirror.* Louis would have painted a viola da gamba at his feet.

The boy looked up from his book and the sudden sadness on his face, or perhaps it was merely boredom, threw a shadow over Louis's heart. He tried to remember his own thoughts at the age of fifteen. But for several months now, forgetfulness, like an octopus, had been spitting its ink around him, and vast stretches of his own past had toppled into the darkness. Memory came back to him only in snatches, in icy, dazzling spurts. He wondered how old Maurice had been when he lost his mother. Did he think about her when he was in boarding school, did he call to her silently from the dormitory on nights when the memory of some unpleasantness suffered during the day, some classmate's taunts, kept him from surrendering to sleep? Louis wished he were brave enough to walk up to that child, who seemed to be another version of himself, and to tell him some true and simple things: things about which we might say later on that we wish someone had told us, comforting words for someone who is standing at the threshold of life and quaking with terror. (But had he himself ever shed that terror?)

The pen Louis held slipped from his fingers and thudded onto the hardwood floor. Maurice emerged from his daydream. With a worried glance at the gap in the curtain, he spied Bapaume. The boy moved his chair so that his back was turned. Geneviève arrived with soup and sandwiches.

Maurice ignored the spoon and drank from the bowl. Steeped in the spontaneous behaviour of childhood, he was inside his body as in a suit that was too big for him. He gorged himself with no ulterior motive, with untroubled greed, in the manner of dogs and little boys. Geneviève sat down at his side and was watching him, smiling. Affection-ately, she tucked away the lock of hair that kept falling onto his forehead.

There was a sound of footsteps on the front stoop. The doorbell rang. Louis couldn't see as far as the vestibule. He pricked up his ears. All he could make out was a confusion of voices.

Geneviève came back shortly. "They've found the verger's daughter."

A man appeared behind her. Already Geneviève was gath-ering up her coat and her rabbit-fur scarf. Maurice gulped his soup and wiped his mouth with the back of his hand.

"They found her in a crevice behind the rocks. It's going to take a while to fish her out."

Bapaume emerged from the living room. "Is she alive?"

Geneviève gazed at him sternly, as if it were none of his business. But it was a legitimate question after all, and she said simply: "They don't know."

Old von Croft materialized at the top of the stairs. He spoke to the man: "Where is the verger?"

"At the presbytery. They convinced him it would be bet-ter if he didn't come along."

The old man grabbed a heavy silver-grey fur coat that hung on a peg. "I'll go and wait with him. And you," he said to his son, who had started buttoning his coat, "I want you to stay here. The dogs are tired, you should be thinking about feeding them. And we can't leave this gentleman all alone in the house. Don't worry, it's not a question of trust, you understand, but one of propriety," he added for the ben-efit of Bapaume, who had gone pale.

Grumbling, Maurice went back to his plate.

"I'll walk, the exercise will be good for me," the old man told his daughter.

Louis was sorry to be the obstacle preventing Maurice from joining the rest of the village; no doubt the boy was annoyed at him now. He felt uneasy too at being involved, despite himself, in a tragedy that didn't concern him. People were bustling all around him, with little concern for his person. Would it be appropriate for him to rush to the crevice, in case they needed as many hands as possible? Should he at least offer to help? But Julia could come back at any moment, he might appear to be contradicting the reason for his visit, which might seem even less justified. . . . He stood there in the middle of the room, a silly and shameless presence, as cumbersome as a heavy piece of furniture.

"I repeat, Julia, I'd rather walk," said the old man.

"After twenty-eight years he still confuses us!" sighed Geneviève.

Louis walked to the door with them. It was as if all at once life were coming back to the village. In the distance, people, mostly women, could be seen pouring out of the houses. They called out to one another, interpreted the latest rumours. They were all running towards the fjord.

Then he spied one woman who wasn't running. She was slowly coming closer. It was the lady he'd seen leaving the general store.

"Shut the door!" Geneviève shouted. "We don't have to heat the outdoors!"

Louis started like a man pulled from his sleep. He went inside at once, shivering from head to toe.

Maurice had finished eating and now, ensconced in an easy chair, was ruminating over his Latin book. Bent down, nostrils flared, he was nibbling on a cinnamon galette. At times his lips moved silently. He blew on the crumbs that fell between the pages. Not once did he lift his nose from the book. He acted as if Bapaume weren't there.

Louis didn't know how to approach him and, as with letters you've delayed replying to for too long, it struck him that any attempt after so much time would seem even more incongruous. With his elbows on the table, he was absent-mindedly peeling clumps of wax off the candlestick.

"You're interested in music, are you?" He decided to go on speaking to the boy in a friendly manner, to act sociable. It sounded so false, however, that his own voice depressed him. It was so like him. He'd never been able to assume a casual manner, even though everyone else around him did. "Who composed the music I saw on your piano?"

Maurice responded with a grimace, as if the question had never occurred to him. "I don't know. Frère Decelles, I think. He's in charge of our school choir. He made us learn it."

"It's magnificent music."

No reaction.

Bapaume guessed that the boy's apparent indifference concealed a reluctance to talk about what was most important to him. "Would you . . . would you mind if I gave it a closer look?"

"I don't care." The boy stuck his nose back in his book.

Louis went to the living room and picked up the score. Over his shoulder, he said: "Oh! I just noticed some pages are missing! . . . There are only seven here."

"That's as far as we studied the piece," retorted Maurice, who, giving in to temptation, furtively sniffed the edge of his book.

Bapaume, who had seen him, sat down at the table again. He noticed that Maurice's leg was shaking constantly in a nervous tremor. "Is it you who annotated it?"

"Excuse me?"

"These annotations on the score, did you make them?" He pointed to them, for the meaning of the word seemed to elude the boy.

"That? No. It was Frère Decelles. I lost my copy. He let me borrow his over the holidays."

"Ah." Bapaume was careful not to let his disappointment show. He spread the sheets in front of him and pretended to be sight-reading but, despite himself, his gaze kept drifting towards the staircase. He wondered if they'd made any changes in the rooms upstairs. At the threshold of Julia's bedroom his imagination backed away, turned around with a shudder, like a fish behind the glass of an aquarium. He struggled to concentrate on the score, but his heart wasn't in it. There were times when even music was too much for him. Music seemed to be one more lie, a pompous inflation of a nursery rhyme that frightened children sing to them-selves in the dark.

Maurice's yawn was like a snake's, long and lazy. His eyes met Bapaume's, which were glued to him; flustered, the boy flung his book onto the table.

"Where are you going?"

"To feed the dogs."

Bapaume couldn't think of a reason to keep him. The boy walked around the house and past the window. His footsteps could be heard in the dry snow. The dogs welcomed him with excited barking.

Louis went back to the living room to gather up the papers he'd written on. He took a blank sheet and, as if he were writing about someone else, jotted down: *He knew it was impossible to pierce the carapace of this boy, this son with whom he felt so many affinities — precisely because he was* endowed with a sensibility like his own. The love he felt for the boy, deep though it was, plunged him into a kind of ecstatic lethargy close to that produced by drugs, and it made him go to pieces. His discomfort, not to say embarrassment, in Maurice's presence was the discomfort, the embarrassment he'd always felt in his relations with himself. But that which he most loathed about himself he took pity on in his fellow creature, feeling sad on his behalf, and he only loved him more for it.

Louis went to the chair where the boy had been sitting and knelt down. He picked up the cushion on which his head had rested. He gazed at it for a long time, buried his face in it, and breathed deeply of it, with his eyes closed. Yes, he thought, pity, sympathy in a costume of fire, was the most violent of human emotions.

A gust of wind threw open the poorly closed door, blowing a gust of icy air inside. Louis stood up. He started when he spied the woman from the general store at the side of the road. She had crouched down and, with the tip of a branch, was drawing pensively in the snow. "The village lunatic," he thought as he closed the door.

Strange though how, all at once, he thought she resembled his mother.

Louis moved the rocking chair over to the window so he could watch for the villagers' return. He ate several galettes, some stewed onions, and fried pork, slowly, realizing he'd eaten almost nothing since the previous day. With his legs wrapped in a blanket, he let a gentle drowsiness come over him. His thoughts drifted away in swirls of smoke. He wondered if the verger's daughter could have survived being buried in the snow for more than thirty-six hours. Her disappearance didn't necessarily mean she was dead, perhaps she was only hurt. Images of Françoise blended with those of the verger's daughter, drifting into his mind all by themselves, without having been summoned (the luxuriant life of her breast and the well of her mouth, her hair that had the scent and colour of charcoal). Through his limbs spread a murmur of memories, like the shuddering of birds beneath the leaves of a sleeping tree.

The clock stopped ticking, and there was something tangible about the sudden silence that drew him from his lethargy. They'd probably forgotten to rewind it. All at once, being in this strange house struck him as odd. The wood fire glanced off the hardwood floor, shimmering purple. More than half an hour had passed and Maurice still wasn't back.

Unless unbeknownst to Bapaume the boy had returned and gone directly upstairs? Louis took an oil lamp and started up. He made his way to the room where a lightbulb was burning. A wasteland: the bed was unmade, and pants, a hockey sweater, and underwear were strewn on the floor that was scattered with rolled-up socks like windfall apples. The room of a schoolboy home for the holidays.

But no Maurice. Louis assumed that the temptation had been too great and that the boy had disobeyed his father and gone to join the rescue squads near the fjord.

It was easy to guess at the love his father bore her by the fact that even though she was married, Julia's room had been left as it was. It was the smallest room upstairs, Julia having always given in on everything. Little had changed. There were a good thirty dolls. Louis had often remarked that whereas boys preserve nothing from their past out of shame for it, girls don't throw anything away; they let their childhood fade in secret, giving it some tender touch-ups now and then.

Everything was carefully stored, in a delicate order. The

walls were covered with photos of Maurice, from the earliest to the most recent. One showed him in a choir, wearing a white surplice. Another, at age six, in a clown costume. In a third, he was kneeling, with a rosary wrapped around his hands, his face turned towards paradise, as if it were something that existed but could not be seen with the eyes.

Louis spied a shadow in the back yard, near the shed. Maurice? He blew out the lamp so he couldn't be seen. In the hallway, he bumped into a small table and there was a sound of papers falling to the floor. He picked them up as best he could and went back downstairs to the dining room.

They were the rest of Frère Decelles's composition. Louis was slightly irritated with Maurice. Why hadn't he told him that these pages were in his possession? At the same time, now that he had them in his hands, Louis was annoyed by them. His state of mind was such that the accomplishments of others reminded him of his own mediocrity, and he had a horror of envy. He overcame his hesitation though, took a seat at the table, and placed the sheets of paper beside the candlestick, among the crumbs of wax.

The piece was twelve pages long, divided into four songs, four brief prayers. The author may have composed it in a weekend, but no matter. It was one of those little things in which an artist is revealed. Louis started reading it to be quite certain, but soon the spell began to work again.

And he went on, bewitched, as if he'd been carried away on a broomstick. The diligence with which it had been retranscribed spoke eloquently of the author's quiet pride, his love, his devotion to his music. Who could he be, this Frère Decelles? Bapaume pictured him in hobnailed boots, a patched soutane, with tape holding his spectacles together, a victim of mockery, his head filled with knowledge as vast as a cathedral. Knowing that his music was being served up to schoolboys numb from sports and lewd daydreams, to parents and colleagues four-fifths of whom couldn't tell an E from a C. And a little inner smile, filled with sadness and irony, resigned to eternal ingratitude.

The finale consisted of a prayer of Atonement. It went well beyond a simple mastery of counterpoint; it was close to grace, to the purity of a heartbreak, and Bapaume felt tears sting his eyes. Yes, Frère Decelles must also know what it is to be buried alive in the coffin of oblivion, in the heavy soil that is the indifference of mankind and of the future. But to persevere all the same, despite knowing that it's impossible to wake the dead, to continue in the face of the exhaustion that follows creativity, spoke of a tenacity and courage that people who do not create, those walking corpses, know nothing of. "I'll write to this Frère Decelles," thought Bapaume.

The work ended in the middle of a page, all the voices in unison at first, then falling one by one like asphyxiated birds, leaving only one that expired on a magnificent held-note. Louis was fascinated, unable to detach himself from the B-flat that suspended the action enigmatically.

Abruptly, he flung the sheet of music onto the table in the same distraught movement with which he would have discarded a bloody knife. At the bottom of the page, a note written in letters so small that he had had to bring it up to his nose to read: *Retranscribed from the Saint-Aldor archives by Frère Adrien Decelles. Composed around 1927 by Monsieur Louis Bapaume, music teacher at the Orphanage of the Crucifixion.*

———

He pushed the door open violently. He headed for the back yard.

"Maurice? . . . Maurice?"

The dogs produced a concert of howling that made Louis recoil, and he tumbled backwards into the logs. His pirouette humiliated him, even without witnesses. He picked up a handful of snow and made a ball which he threw in the direction of the dogs. The barking intensified. He dispatched a second one. Then he took handfuls of snow which he flung onto his head, scrubbing his face and neck furiously, for no reason, as if to defy the order of things through acts that made no sense at all.

He paused on the doorstep. He had the feeling that he wasn't being taken seriously. He'd been left there by the others who had more important things to deal with! They were tolerating his presence without much concern, as if he were some harmless idiot being left to his obsessions. What use had his scruples been these past months, and his descent into the depths of hell and of the heart, if he was to be treated like this by a village of ignoramuses? He had broken himself into pieces of his own free will, like someone smashing open a piggybank; he had offered up his talent as a sacrifice — and who among them could measure the extent of that immolation? As his revolt erupted, Louis felt tempted to let everything drop, contemptuously, and leave straightaway with no explanation.

But it was also a temptation to run from his self-imposed duty; he knew that, and he balked, stiffening his resolve. He would keep his word with himself. More selfishness, more vanity? Too bad. He felt unable to wait one more minute. He resolved to go to the village and wait at the hotel, at the church, in the middle of the road, anywhere. His watch showed 4:15; he would return to the von Crofts' around 6:00. He considered leaving them a note, but then he picked up his case and his coat and hat, and left. The mere thought of putting words on paper made him feel like vomiting.

The church steeple came into sight at the top of the hill, a five-minute walk away. Bapaume crossed the field and got back on the road. He went along at a stubborn pace, cursing between his teeth. The same breath of wind swept the snow at ground level and bent the tops of the trees, confused the clattering of branches and the music of the stars. Bapaume wanted to shout at the wind to be quiet. An orange glow rose above the hill and accentuated its contour, just as if someone had lit a fire behind a wall.

On the other side of the road, ahead of him, a silhouette was heading for the village. He could barely make it out but guessed from the pace that it was Maurice. He called out. The silhouette didn't turn around. Louis walked faster to catch up with the boy, but as he moved forward the road started to climb uphill, and soon it was so steep he had to stop to get his breath back. "Wait! I've got something to tell you!"

But the boy was walking faster and faster, almost as if he were running away. Making one last effort, Bapaume began to run. He finally put his hand on the other's shoulder. Only then did he realize his mistake. The child was very small, he couldn't be more than twelve. He tried to break away but Louis was holding on to his fur collar.

"Help me, I'm going to faint." He made it up the final stretch of the hill by leaning on the child. He pulled the boy off the road and, carried along by his own weight, wobbled like a hoop at the end of its run, and collapsed at the foot of a tree. "You aren't Maurice," he said, out of breath and half-delirious.

"No, Monsieur, my name's Gérard."

Leaning against the tree trunk, Bapaume tried to smile,

despite the grimaces provoked by his blazing lungs. "Tell me, what are you? A porcupine?"

"I don't understand, Monsieur."

"Never mind . . . it doesn't matter," said Louis, feebly waving his hand.

The little boy gazed at the traveller with the serious look that children have when they feel that something is getting away from them. He brought his mittens close to Louis's face and placed them over the man's ears to warm them.

"Ah, I see, you're a good Samaritan, is that it?"

"A good Montagnais, Monsieur."

"You're right, you're right. It's only among the Montagnais that porcupines are called Gérard."

The boy was leaning towards him slightly and Louis saw him with the heavens as a background. Blood was pounding in his temples, clouding his vision, multiplying the stars, lighting up others in the child's hair. He closed his eyes to ease the panic he could feel inside his chest. He waved Gérard away. He thought he was about to die of exhaustion. The prospect didn't frighten him. After all, if his corpse were to be found the next day, petrified in its enigma. . . . No one would understand why this man had come here to die, the von Crofts least of all. It would be a sneaky revenge but Bapaume pushed aside the temptation. He opened his eyes. The young Montagnais was no longer there.

And then Louis let out a startled cry. Suddenly, very close to his face, was the most horrifying thing he'd ever seen. A kind of hideous wound full of teeth and with bulging eyes. Scared away by his cry, the thing disappeared into the ditch. He saw a low black form crawling away. He had no idea what it could be. He straightened up, still trembling. He dusted the snow and mud off his clothes. Cautiously, he took a few steps, afraid of encountering the abomination again, and passed through a curtain of evergreens. And then, suddenly, the village appeared at his feet, sparkling like a kingdom.

The inhabitants were gathered around the church. The sharp cold made clear the light from their torches. Bapaume couldn't see what they were looking at. But given the gravity of their silence, it seemed as if an angel with broken wings had just fallen to earth at this very place. Louis could have stayed till morning gazing at the beauty of his vision. But curiosity won out and he hurtled down the gentle slope to the graveyard, which was an extension of the church property.

The crowd was scattered into small groups from which came only brief whispers. Louis didn't know what everyone was waiting for. A few individuals went up to the church and ventured just past the threshold. Then they'd go back to the groups, make a quick remark *sotto voce*, and once again become silent. They stared at Bapaume with the look of curiosity and mistrust with which strangers are regarded in places where few are seen. The temperature continued to drop. Louis's limbs were growing numb. The lights in the church called to him with the promise of warmth. A murmur spread around him just as he started up the steps. He didn't care, he was too cold.

The plank coffin had been placed at the transept crossing. It was surrounded by four candles. Louis advanced slowly. He barely noticed old von Croft placing a consoling hand on the verger's neck. The latter, sitting on a straight-backed chair, dumbfounded with pain, gazed uncomprehendingly at what was left of the flesh of his flesh. Bapaume went to a pew on the side aisle. He let himself drop to his knees, with no intention of praying; fatigue and dismay were simply depriving him of the use of his legs. His lips quivered in a sort of silent mumbling. Nothing takes up more space in a church than a doll's coffin, white as the vast snow.

THE TEDDY BEAR

THE LITTLE GIRL APPEARED to be eight or nine years old. The still-frozen folds of her skirt spilled from the narrow box. A delicate mist enveloped her body and, in the warmth from the candles placed at either end of the coffin, delicate curls of steam rose from her blonde hair and her moccasins. Her translucent skin had strange glimmers, pale and blue, pretty, even, like mother-of-pearl. You wanted to take her in your arms to keep her warm. Under her slightly raised head — perhaps her neck had been broken — someone had slipped a white cushion. Her little fists were close to her chin, clutching the collar of her parka as if, from the depths of death and for all eternity, she still shivered from terror and cold.

Old von Croft waved vaguely at Louis, as his father had waved in his dream the night before. Then he realized that the other man was actually telling him to take off his hat. Louis did so, flushing. The organ began to murmur very softly in the loft, as in the mountains when you approach a stream. And at the third measure Bapaume wondered if he was losing his mind.

He walked up to the little dead girl and placed one knee on the floor. From close up she was even more terrifying. A rosary had been wrapped around her wrist. A last bit of hoarfrost was melting in the folds of her clothing, dried blisters covered the skin around her nostrils and lips, like burns. Bapaume was forced to look away because her eyelids were slightly open, as if she were about to wake up, and they made her even more beautiful.

Louis brought his hands together. But the music coming from the organ caused him such anguish, it was impossible for him to feign prayer. He made his way to the back of the church, careful to tiptoe on the floor tiles. The verger, who until then had seemed unaware of his presence, gave the stranger a look of grim surprise. Louis was afraid of being addressed at any moment. ("What are you doing here? You've got no business! Who do you think you are?") The wooden steps creaked under his weight. The organ was the work of an artisan, a genuine ambassador of God on earth whom no one remembered. Bapaume had once known the instrument inside and out. He knew he could gather around him a choir of seraphim that would come forthwith from the four corners of paradise. Beyond the choir loft there was another set of stairs to climb. Louis arrived just as the piece finished. The lady from the general store was at the keyboard.

She kept her face impassive, like someone who's prepared for what is about to happen. Louis stopped in the middle of the staircase with only his head and shoulders protruding from the trapdoor. The organist spied him out of the corner of her eye. She brought her hands to her face and wearily rubbed her high cheekbones, pulled at the skin of her cheeks, and joined her hands behind her neck. Then her wrists dropped limply onto her thighs. Bapaume climbed up the final stairs.

"What's the meaning of this? How do you know that music? It's never been published. I wrote it over twenty years ago, in Paris!" All said hurriedly, in a frightened whisper.

"There was a time when you were a lot friendlier, Monsieur Bapaume."

Louis stood there, bewildered. He studied the woman's face. Aside from its resemblance to his mother's, it said nothing to him; he would have sworn he'd never seen it before today. "I think you're saying that we knew each other once.

But . . . I'm sorry . . . I have no memory of you." He was bent over slightly, his fist on his chest, his features expressing the most sincere dismay. "You're saying that I was the one who taught you that music, Madame?"

She let him meditate on that for a few seconds. Then, with calculated indifference, she said: "I transposed it for piano, didn't I? I'm amazed you've forgotten. We played it as a duet, when we got out of bed, the last morning we were together. Remember. It was just before you left."

"Really, Madame? Really?" He sat on the bench, appalled. He shook his head. He made some vague motions with his hands, which came to nothing. He looked like a man who'd just been told of a disaster. "One of the first pieces I wrote. I couldn't have been more than twenty. It's from the period — from the blessed time — when I com- posed without thinking, the way a beaver builds dams with no idea of the harm it could cause. I mean . . . do you think a Koch bacillus knows what it's doing? I'm asking you very seriously, Madame. If you were a Koch bacillus, would you have any clear idea of the harm you were causing?"

"Well, I don't know. No. I don't think so."

She was staring at him uneasily, suspiciously, the way you look at someone who's not quite right in the head, and Bapaume was aware of it. He looked down again.

He seemed to be speaking just to himself. "It's silly, but I'd completely forgotten that piece. . . . Yes, one of the very first ones I composed. I was amazed to find the manuscript last summer . . . I'd decided to make it the beginning of my oratorio." He looked up at her. "Yes, I was composing an oratorio, if you can imagine. I'm not joking, Madame. I was a man who was humiliated, unappreciated, almost destroyed by the worst tragedy that can befall a human being. And it was while I was working on that introduction that I suddenly realized all my efforts . . . well, it doesn't matter. I was punished for my pride. Music has left me forever, Madame. Indeed, is there anyone who's interested in such things? All this must sound incoherent and I can see that I'm boring you . . ."

"You aren't boring me."

"If I have caused you any harm. . . . It would be even more serious if I'd forgotten all about it . . ."

The woman made no reply. Nothing showed in her attitude but a weary understanding and a sorrow that had seen it all before, that expects nothing much from the world or from what individuals try to do for one another. Slowly, she walked past Bapaume and picked up her purse from the other end of the bench. From it she took two cloth bags. "Here," she said.

It was as if he hadn't heard her. With a crazed look, he grabbed her arm. And concentrating entirely on his outburst, like a man who is fervently confessing a sin: "I thought it was a woman!"

The musician raised her eyebrows. Gently she released her wrist from Bapaume's grip. "What are you talking about?"

"The little dead girl behind the rocks! I didn't know. I thought it was a woman! Do you understand? An adult, not a little girl! And why have they exposed her like that, in the state she was found in? Shouldn't the dead be clothed?"

"It's what the verger wanted. I don't know why." She paused, then added that she'd been the girl's teacher. That she was a lovely child. That she'd rather not talk about her. Outside, you could hear the sound of the crowd beginning to move, the creaking of boots on the snow.

"You must have been very fond of her, Madame, if you don't want to talk about her."

Again the woman said: "Here!" and held out the two

small bags. Bapaume took them and examined them, uncomprehending.

From her purse the woman took a package of cigarettes and lit one with feigned nonchalance. Bapaume looked at her, stunned. Smoking in a church! She was trying to look natural, but she obviously wasn't used to tobacco. As soon as she had some smoke in her mouth she expelled it, without inhaling, with an involuntary grimace, and tears came to her eyes. "I was twenty-four years old. It's strange now to think that I could have been twenty-four once. You would turn up at nightfall, once a week, sometimes twice, when you came back from teaching the little von Croft twins. I didn't see enough of you and sometimes I took risks. I'd prowl around the von Croft house just so I could get a look at you from a distance, through a window. I didn't dare go out, I was so haunted by the painful hope that you might turn up unexpectedly. You'd come by the back yard to be sure you wouldn't be seen and you'd stay till dawn. And on that particular morning I'd told myself: 'So he's forgotten something again!' And I took these two objects and put them in my purse so I could give them back to you the next time we met. My only mistake was thinking that I'd see you that same day. But then early that evening someone told me you'd left. Still, I knew that we'd meet eventually, because I simply couldn't imagine that you'd leave without saying goodbye. For twenty years now I've never stepped outside without them . . ."

Bapaume, alarmed, fingered the bags without opening them. "What are these?"

"When I saw you today I thought for a moment . . . how can I put it? I thought you'd come back because of me. A little, anyway. To ask my forgiveness. Why are you looking at me like that all of a sudden?"

He didn't reply.

Embarrassed, she ground the cigarette under her heel. Not knowing what to do with the butt, she put it back inside the package.

The first bag held a pipe, the second a hard glass object, pyramid-shaped. A prism perhaps. There wasn't enough light to be certain. Vaguely, very vaguely, Louis recalled that in the distant past he'd tried tobacco. The glass pyramid could have belonged to anyone.

"You left one on the bedside table, the other in the ashtray in the kitchen." These words were things that she dropped nonchalantly along her way. She went back to the organ.

The trapdoor opened, a little old lady appeared, and, because her black dress was wrapped in darkness, it seemed as if an ancient white head was floating in the air. She carried some scores which she placed slowly on the music stand. The organist thanked her. The old lady said something to her in an undertone and the other woman responded in the same way.

The crowd outside finally began to surge into the church but Louis couldn't imagine for what sudden reason. He leaned over the railing.

"It's the last rescue team coming back," the musician explained. "The priest was with them. He's the one they've been waiting for."

Her hands approached the keyboards. The old lady was sitting obediently at her side to turn pages.

"I realize that you must have suffered because of me. I do regret it, believe me. Forgive me too for having completely forgotten. I . . . if you only knew . . . fate has dealt me a terrible blow."

She snickered briefly, bitterly. "Go in peace, as they say;

I'm not angry with you. The two of us have nothing more to say to each other."

He walked up to her, hesitantly.

"Please excuse me, Monsieur Bapaume," she said in a firm and steady voice, and it sounded like an order.

Louis withdrew. Without his being aware of it, she watched him till he'd disappeared in the stairwell. He considered leaving the pipe and the glass object behind on the step but then thought better of it and stowed them in his pocket. He pricked up his ears. Once again, the music resounding in the church was his.

"Louise, something like yours," she would have told him. But he hadn't even thought to ask her name.

The multitude was making its way among the pews, in a sort of contemplative movement, the way that you limit your movements in a bedroom at night so as not to wake a sleeping child. People from the wider area had probably come to offer their condolences, for it was unlikely that the population of Saint-Aldor was this large. A young priest was making his way to the coffin with incredulous circumspection, overwhelmed by pity and sorrow. A heavy scarf was tied around his neck; he was squeezing his beret in his right fist. Bapaume heard someone murmur: "He's the one who taught her to read . . ."

He spotted Maurice von Croft talking with his father at the entrance to the nave. They, in turn, noticed him and started walking towards him. But the boy stopped midway there and went out through the lateral door.

Robert von Croft's eyes were red and swollen. "My son tells me that the woman has delivered. Julia asked him to say that she's prepared to see you. She is still at the Soucys'. It's very close to here, across from the general store: the green house, you can't miss it. Julia's expecting you."

Candles passed from one parishioner to the next, each person lighting a candle from a neighbour's flame. The young priest joined the verger and, despondent, pressed his forehead against the prie-dieu. Groups of children guided by their teachers entered in close order. They were of all ages. The youngest were dressed like teddy bears. One could be seen clapping his hands: he thought it was the Christmas celebration. Louis looked for the little Montagnais boy, but he didn't seem to be there. The flames of the candles around the coffin began to dance slowly, as if the little girl were in a dream.

The old man held on to Louis's sleeve. "I've told Maurice to get the horses and sleigh ready. He'll drive you to the station. You mustn't dawdle, but you should be all right for eight o'clock."

"Thank you for everything, Monsieur von Croft."

He looked Bapaume squarely in the eyes. "You know, Monsieur Bapaume, I'm a conscientious craftsman. I can tell a piece of wood I'll use to make a piece of furniture from one that will end up in the fire. It's the same with forgetfulness. What I mean is . . . it knows what it's doing when it throws something into the fire."

Bapaume humbly nodded his assent. "I'll try not to forget that."

Von Croft went on staring at him with his impenetrable gaze but said nothing more.

"What right do I have to bother these people?" Louis thought. His presence in the village struck him as more and more incongruous, unjustifiable, absurd.

He shut the door of the church behind him just as they

were beginning the first prayer. The general store was straight ahead, at the bottom of the hill. He was neither nervous nor frightened. Both his head and his heart felt empty. He was on his way to a self-imposed duty, and wouldn't question himself anymore. Still, he couldn't suppress a shudder when he first spied the green house. From the church, the organ's rumbling sent a vibration through the ground that spread to his legs.

The door opened just as he stepped onto the path in the front yard. Julia was giving some advice to a man who was standing on the threshold. He showed his fervour and his gratitude by kissing her hands.

Immediately after that, she turned to Louis: "If it isn't Monsieur Bapaume!" she said cheerfully. "Of all people!"

Tears came to his eyes, uncontrollable, and he murmured her name.

She moved closer to him, radiant, holding out her hand. "So. I understand you want to talk to me." It was Julia as God must have designed her for all eternity. As she'd been at the age of eight. As she would be on Judgment Day.

"A big seven-pound baby," she said, gesturing over her shoulder to the Soucys' house. "A little girl."

"Congratulations."

She gave a good-natured laugh. "Oh, I'm not the one to congratulate . . ."

Then she observed him with her intense, luminous eyes. Just as they'd been in the past with that glimmer of anxiety deep down, as if she were watching a tightrope walker, alert to the slightest quiver in the rope. Louis looked tenderly at the beauty spot above her lip.

"What have you come here to tell me, Monsieur Bapaume?"

He hesitated, looking like a child who doesn't know if

he's done a good deed or something wrong.

She stroked Louis's sweaty forehead with her fingertips. "You still have soot under your eyes. Put your hat on, you're liable to catch cold."

"I came to ask your forgiveness, Julia."

"Forgiveness? For what?" She spoke in a murmur.

Louis squeezed his eyes shut and buried his face in his scarf.

"Come, let's not stand outside here." Gently, she took him by the elbow. "We'll walk towards the church. It always does us good to walk to church."

Louis Bapaume went along with her. He hadn't taken five steps when his knees gave out and he collapsed into some bushes covered with frost. His scraped cheek was bleeding.

"You shouldn't let yourself get into such a state."

Louis was taking deep breaths. "I'm all right, Mademoiselle von Croft. Don't worry about me."

"I'm not Mademoiselle von Croft anymore, I'm Madame Rocheleau."

"I'm sorry, I'll remember."

"Goodness, it isn't serious."

Bapaume was looking at the snow as he walked. He could feel Julia's arm linked with his and he was wishing that he didn't have to say what he had to say. How dear her presence was to him! And how good it would have been to walk like this, side by side, for no other reason than the joy of seeing each other again!

"Are you going to tell me what —"

"I behaved very badly with you. I acted in a way no one should be allowed to act with children."

They continued walking in silence. Julia was thinking.

"Try as I may," she said finally, "I swear I don't understand."

They were near the church now. Julia went to the door and, standing on tiptoe, she ventured a glance through the window. A minute's silence was being observed. Everyone had knelt to pray. The candles sparkled above their heads like a carpet of stars. She sat down on the top step.

"I was harsh with you. I slapped you on the head. One time, I can still remember . . . I took the ruler and . . . and I struck you ten times on your legs. Ten times!"

Julia burst out laughing. "Oh, that! I remember! But I deserved it, for heaven's sake. Wasn't that the time my sister and I tried to pass for one another? Lots of twins like doing that, especially as children; they don't mean any harm. But you weren't so easily fooled, you knew which was which by the way we played the piano. That day I saw that you'd lost your composure."

"But I still had no right to do it!"

"Very well, let's admit it wasn't very nice of you. Do you want me to scold you? All right, you behaved very badly that day, so there! There, it's done. Are we even now?"

Louis Bapaume brought his fists to his temples. "I'm not joking, Mademoiselle von Croft! What I did was serious, very serious. I abused my role. Don't you see? Dear God, if I have to explain it all . . . I was the laughing stock of Saint-Aldor School. My pupils baited me, the other teachers didn't support me and openly made fun of my attempts to teach music; they ridiculed the method I'd devised! It was all silly, I agree, and I realized it soon enough. But my lifelong dream was collapsing. And no one helped me. Not one little bit. No one."

Julia examined this worn-out man who was prematurely old and perhaps sick. He seemed to be nearly out of breath. It was the last thing she'd have expected. Never for a moment would she have thought that his actions, which he saw as crimes, were sins. But perhaps she was mistaken. The zeal with which he blamed himself was so impressive, and in a way so suspect, that a doubt was sown in Julia's heart, one that she couldn't shed.

Bapaume had put down his case. He was pacing, his hands crossed behind his back. Then, coming to a halt: "And then there was you. You, Julia, who had such a gift for music. And I clung to you as to a life belt! With your grace, your intelligence, your vivacity, you made up for all the hours of humiliation I'd lived through at the school. And I loved you, Julia! Dear God, how I loved you! Did you realize that? Did you know that I'd come at night and climb up onto the roof so I could watch you through your window as you slept? Yes, I did that: I, Louis Bapaume, I did that!" He struck his chest with his fist, uncertain whether it was a bitter reproach addressed to himself or an arrogant affirmation. "And I prayed for you, Julia. Every morning, every evening. I thought that praying would ward off disaster. I was absolutely out of my mind. I composed little pieces in your range. All those things I used to make you play were mine! I'd composed them just for you!" And he began to hum a gay, jaunty tune, beating time with his arms, prrrom-pom-pa-pom, prrrom-pom-pa-pom. He interrupted himself abruptly. "That whole period is very confused in my mind. I was trying then to convince myself that everything was illusion — matter, the world, something along those lines. I spent exhausting nights doing nothing else. I'd arrive at your house at the appointed hour, worn out, half my head in orbit; only music could bring me back to earth. And you, you were having *fun!* You treated your musical talent like . . . like some old toy you were tired of. You neglected your lessons, you'd heave great sighs of boredom, you and your sister would snicker behind my back at the way I dressed or at certain words that made me stammer. That was why I saw red!"

"Please, I beg you, calm down," she said gently.

"I came to ask your forgiveness for all that."

Singing mixed with murmurs could be heard again; the bell began to toll. Bapaume jumped so suddenly he nearly lost his balance.

"Dear God! There's no need to be frightened like that. It's just Coq-l'Oeil."

The poor animal was hideous. Half his face was missing; there was no skin to cover his jaw, and one eye, which was the size of a golf ball, barely held on to the edge of his skull, and threatened to roll to the ground as it darted its fossil-like gaze, distraught and purple, up to the heavens. Louis recognized him as the thing he'd seen on the road a while before.

"The beggar's dog," said Julia, stroking its neck. "Someone, no one knows who, threw boiling oil in his face one day. And this is the result. It was such a shock to his master, he passed away that same night. These things do happen, you know. Since then, Coq-l'Oeil hasn't belonged to anyone, and pretty well everybody feeds him. He turns up with no warning every three months. He'll spend a few days with us, plying his master's noble trade, then go away again, looking as if he understands things that we don't. You aren't much to look at, but it's not your fault, is it Coq-l'Oeil?" She rubbed her cheek against the dog's neck. "But still. Feel how soft his fur is. Like a cloud."

Louis didn't move.

"I promise you, Monsieur Bapaume, he isn't vicious. If you're vicious you get a better deal than that from life, believe me."

"Animals terrify me. I've never touched a dog in my life."

"You don't have a gift for happiness." She went on

petting Coq-l'Oeil with her mitten. "You mentioned hitting me on the head, Monsieur Bapaume. But as far as I recall, when you did, it was just with a few sheets of paper — nothing that could cut my head open." Laughing, she added: "My skull's a lot thicker than that, isn't it Coq-l'Oeil? Now it's true, there was that time later on when you struck me on the legs with the ruler. There was also a time when I laughed during one of your musical dictations — you used to call them note races — and you made me stay on my knees with my wrists tied behind my back, and maybe the ties were a little tight . . ."

His eyes shut, Louis Bapaume chewed on his fist.

"But that," she hastened to add, "I can still remember laughing about the next day. And what else was there? What do you have to reproach yourself for? Look at me, Monsieur Bapaume. At the time I never would have thought you were so unhappy. I'm the one who should be asking your forgiveness."

"Don't say that, I beg you. Don't say that. Your sister hasn't forgotten what I subjected you to. I can see that she's still angry with me."

"Oh, that. My sister may have been in a bad mood this afternoon, but she's like that with anyone who approaches me; she sees me as her property in a way."

"As far as I can tell, Geneviève already hated me twenty years ago."

"Don't think that," she said, in a voice that held surprise and compassion. "I know my sister, as you may imagine. And perhaps back then you only had eyes for her twin. You barely noticed her own efforts. She'd sit in her corner watching us, particularly you, I think. Twenty years later you come back, and again it's her sister you want to talk to. Geneviève may have suffered because of it, I don't know."

"So there too, I was acting unjustly . . ."

"No, you weren't."

The dog stood on his hind paws and Louis recoiled. Then, just like that, the animal trotted away. Bapaume gathered up his case. He held it against his belly.

"What else do you have to tell me, Monsieur Bapaume? I'm tired. I can see a question in your eyes."

"Music? Do you still . . . ?"

Julia didn't answer him right away. With a hint of vexation and pity for him, as if despite the sorrow she regretted having to cause him she had to play her role to the end, she pulled off her mitten. The three end fingers of her left hand had been cut off. "An accident," she said. And after a detached sniff, she put the mitten back on.

Bapaume was as still as a statue. His features were frozen. Then, like a drop from the tip of an icicle, a tear suddenly welled up in the corner of his eye, slipped slowly to his chin, and turned white. The organ and the singing had started up again inside the church. In a voice she could barely recognize, one that came from the heart, with the emphasis one gives to words that will be spoken only once in one's lifetime, he said: "I swear, Julia, no matter what unforgivable punishments I inflicted on you, never for one second did I experience the slightest pleasure."

From Julia came a dry, nervous sob, like a guffaw. She apologized, pleading fatigue. Then wiped her brow with her sleeve. The sincerity of his words freed her of her one suspicion and she breathed more easily. For a moment her attention went beyond Bapaume. The dull, muffled sound of hooves in the snow. Maurice in the distance, with the horses and sleigh.

"And you've come all this way, after twenty years, to talk about that. I swear, if I'd known . . ."

Louis sat near her on a lower step. His face was level with Julia's thighs. She was suddenly pensive.

"They're going to call her Carmen."

"Sorry?"

"The Soucy family. The little girl who was just born — they're going to call her Carmen. The name of the verger's daughter."

"I had a son," said Louis. "He was twelve years old. He passed away last spring."

Julia looked in the direction of the Soucy house. Her eyes glowed as if someone were moving a candle in front of them. The words couldn't come to her lips, they fell back into her heart, stillborn. Finally she took hold of Bapaume's hand and placed her cheek against it. Louis's hand was warm, hairy, damp, and icy at the fingertips, like a dog's muzzle.

"My wife and I had accepted poverty. It was the price of my freedom. She wanted me to think about nothing but music. We lived in a kind of happy and sordid indifference, with dust, a stinking pantry, humidity and mould accumulating in the corners. With all that, no sense of priorities: the costliest liqueurs but holes in our socks; my son reading music at the age of six but unable to read words till much later, almost by chance, hardly going to school — he was talented, the little rascal. There were mice in the house too. I don't know why I'm telling you all this, they didn't inspire any great works; rather, fear and disgust. We were so short of money that we'd sneak into the neighbours' sheds at night to stock up on mousetraps. Of course my wife had her fits of domesticity, her short-lived enthusiasm for a grand reform, and for three days a whirlwind of scrub brushes and steel wool would lay waste to the house. Then we'd weary of it and everything would begin again to droop, to gape, to rot amid all the innocence of happiness. All that to tell you how my son grew up. Before he took sick. And then everything fell apart, a genuine clamour. Nothing is as costly as a child who's going to die. Tuberculosis isn't made for small budgets. We did what we could. Yet I never stop thinking that if I'd taken the teacher's job I was offered five years ago . . . or if we'd given my son living conditions that were, let's say, more reasonable, healthier . . ."

"You shouldn't reproach yourself like that," she murmured.

She was still holding his hand. He felt her warm breath on his palm.

"I . . . for a long time I thought the ordeal was sent by God to call me back to order, to pull me out of the inertia in which I was languishing, out of my inability for two years to compose a single bar of music. So I threw myself into my work. Can you understand? I thought that God expected me to compose a magnificent oratorio inspired by my pain . . . that God would buy a few pages of music with my child's life. But it was my vanity, the demon of my vanity actually, that whispered that to me. . . . Before my son was born, I didn't know what a child was. Having a child teaches us nothing else, but it's enough, it's infinite. I would never have tolerated someone doing to him what I did to you. That's why I got the idea of settling the debt I owed you." He opened his bag, his movements marked with tenderness and calm. "I'd like you to accept this, Julia."

Shivering, Julia brought her hands to her chest, as if she dared not touch what she was being offered: a teddy bear. Its belly had been mended with coarse thread. There was a trouser button in place of the right eye and one ear had been torn off.

"This is the teddy bear my son had when he was very small. He played with it so much that, as you can see, the belly was torn, and it lost an eye, an ear. He mended it himself, I remember; he swiped a trouser button from me. . . . Julia, grant me the favour of taking it."

"But Monsieur Bapaume, I'd never dare . . ."

"Take it. Then and only then will I be able to believe that you've forgiven me."

Julia gave him a questioning look, then nodded gravely. She had just understood the meaning of this gift. She propped the teddy bear against her breast.

"Now don't think I told you all that by way of complaining. Airs and postures I've long ago tossed out the window. In spite of what I've told you, Mademoiselle, I want you to know that we were a happy family, in love with ourselves, a single temperament circulating among the three of us. We were crazy about one another. My son lacked many things, but he never lacked that which cannot be bought. If I had one regret, it would be my inability to find the words to tell him what he meant. . . . But perhaps all fathers are like that."

The sleigh arrived, Maurice jumped out.

"I would also like . . . because I wasn't able to do it myself . . . I would like you to offer my condolences to the verger. Tell him that I too . . . what he is feeling . . ."

"I'll do it without fail, I swear I will." She burst into tears. "Dear God, what have I done?" she asked. "And how cruel we all were to you."

Bapaume untied his scarf and used it to wipe her eyes. "Don't be silly."

She made an effort to smile. "Why not stay? We could all have supper together. There'd even be a bed for you. My father adores talking about the past. I'd like . . . I would like to make amends for —"

"It's impossible, believe me."

She hesitated, then said: "There's something I want to

tell you too . . ." She gave Maurice a questioning look. Louis caught a glimpse of the boy discreetly shaking his head. "Perhaps it's not necessary after all . . ."

There was a silence. She brought her hand up to his face and then — Maurice brandished his whip, the horses shook their bits — with an affectionate simplicity that touched him deeply, she pinched Louis's cheek.

"I was very fond of you too, you know, Monsieur Bapaume. You were so shy, so touching! And I think now that . . . that you've been wonderfully brave. Excuse me, I'm like Coq-l'Oeil, I don't know how to talk. But I shall never forget you. You're the best man I've ever known."

"Oh, don't think that!" he said, then turned on his heel as if to run away from what she'd just said. He stopped short when he found himself facing the dog. They eyed one another. The animal wagged its tail; Bapaume bent down. Shyly, he petted its head. Then Coq-l'Oeil trotted over to Julia.

In small groups, the faithful were leaving the church. The organ had started up again. The music was still Bapaume's. The bass notes pounded against the steps like a heart inside a chest. Maurice helped Louis into the sleigh.

"God be with you!" exclaimed Julia, who was already melting into the crowd.

Bapaume merely gave a disapproving nod as if the last thing he wanted was for God to get involved in all this.

"There," he thought, "the deed is done." And yet, what exactly had been done? He couldn't claim to be relieved, couldn't even talk about an event. He'd done what had to be done, certainly. He'd talked like a torrent, as he'd never talked to anyone before. He was overcome by a feeling of unreality, of stupor, the kind one feels after a funeral.

He sat next to Maurice, their elbows and knees touching. He had just revealed to the boy that he was the composer of the piece that Frère Decelles was rehearsing with the choir, but Maurice had shown no particular reaction; perhaps he hadn't even believed him. The boy only turned his attention from the horses' rumps to scan the horizon, like a sailor reading the sea. "Still, my trip here hasn't been useless," thought Bapaume, "it all has to mean something." He felt within inches of his goal but still unable to touch it. As if all the lamps were in place and he only had to find the switch and there would be light. What was it that Julia had wanted to tell him? And why hadn't Maurice wanted her to?

He studied the boy as if the answer might be hidden on his face, in those eyes as thin as the crack of light underneath a closed door. But his face, like his father's, was made to conceal. Trying to read it was like trying to guess a person's voice by peering at his photo. "Did you know the verger's daughter?"

"A little, like everybody else." He clicked his tongue to wake the horses, who were relaxing.

Filaments of brightness were rising over the mountains, blurring the field of stars as they danced. A few windows were lit up in Saint-Aldor School. At the sight of it, Louis experienced again the humiliation he'd felt when he arrived this morning. In any case, he knew before he even set out that his act would not heal him of himself. It certainly wasn't to feel better afterwards that he'd come all this way to beg forgiveness.

"You know, you remind me a lot of myself when I was your age. I was also a boarder in a school. I never complained. My only havens were silence and music." Bapaume was shivering, but not from cold. He felt as if he were talking to a pile of stones. How the hell could he get through to the boy? Was there any way he could touch him? And how time was flying! He felt an urge to shake him by the shoulders. He looked at his watch and realized he'd lost a glove and didn't know when or where. He stuffed his hand in his pocket and felt something icy cold. It was the little glass pyramid the woman at the church had given him. He'd already forgotten about it.

"Funny, your name is Maurice like my son's. He'd have been thirteen yesterday, December 22."

"Giddy up!"

The horses sped up. They took the path through the woods in the opposite direction from the morning and, once again, snow was falling from the branches in heavy, soft clumps.

As a last attempt, Louis was about to venture a question about the boy's mother, to oblige him to open up, even at the risk of hurting him. One very simple consideration stopped him, however. At the von Crofts' he'd seen no sign of Maurice's mother. Not a single image, no framed photo, no souvenir, nothing! How could it be? And why all those photos of him on the walls of Julia's bedroom when he'd seen none anywhere else? He didn't have enough material to draw any conclusions, he knew that. But having those two facts side by side struck him suddenly as luminous. All at once he felt a certainty — irrational, visceral, dazzling — like the roulette player who knows that the ball is going to stop on his number.

They came to the narrow road that lay along the small valley. About thirty yards away they spied a group of men on snowshoes, carrying torches. It was the troop sent by Lieutenant Hurtubise returning to the railway station. Maurice didn't slow the sleigh. The group had to move to the sides of the road to let them pass.

The von Croft boy stopped the team when it got to the automobile that had been in the ditch since the day before. What was the meaning of this? Bapaume gave the boy a smile that could break your heart. This was a joke, wasn't it?

"You get off here."

"Here? Why? There's more than a mile left. Look, it's already 8:05. Lieutenant Hurtubise can't make the train wait indefinitely. And with all this snow I'll never be able to —"

"This is where they told me to let you off. Here where the road dips."

"Oh?" There was no doubt in his mind that "they" meant Geneviève. "I understand," he said, and got out.

The boy gave him back the blanket.

"Wait just a minute. I . . . I'm afraid you've been told things about me. It's not that they're false. But you know, we can be unfair sometimes in the way we present facts. It would take too long to explain to you. Maybe I'll write you one day. Would you let me do that, Maurice?"

The boy didn't commit himself.

Bapaume's smile was odd, sickly sweet, and sly. "Do you know what just occurred to me?" he asked, blinking. "If God were to come back to earth, what do you think He'd do?"

Maurice looked at him warily. He kept his jaws clenched.

"Very well," said Bapaume, "I think the first thing He'd do would be to ask forgiveness."

Snowflakes were spinning in the light breeze. They flew in every direction like mosquitoes. Some touched down on Maurice's red skin and died there. The boy sighed as if to say: "That story of yours isn't even funny."

"I'd like you to bear this in mind." Bapaume searched for

his words in the snow at his feet, then high above in the dictionary of the stars. "Whatever you've done or think you've done, Maurice, you have the right to breathe. No more and no less than anyone else. You don't have to feel guilty for existing, you don't have to be ashamed. It's that . . . there's no sin that justifies the punishment of watching those we love die. It's not our fault if, for no particular reason, we survive those who are more worthy of living. Do you understand? We are given life without our asking for it and then, when we'd like to bestow it, we can't. *Nothing belongs to us.* No one knows why. But that's the way it is."

Maurice had pulled off his mittens. He was gazing at his fingers, twisting them slowly, with a sort of affection. His timid eyes met Bapaume's and, for the first time that day, Louis thought he could spot a fraternal glimmer there.

"Julia is your mother, isn't she? She had you as a young girl, before she was married, didn't she? Isn't that what she wanted to tell me just now?"

The whistle of a locomotive could be heard in the distance.

"What does it matter?" Bapaume wondered. He was thinking that Julia had wanted to reveal that secret to him out of compassion, to say that she also knew what it was to have a child, to cherish a human being outside oneself, and it seemed to him that because of that — if only because of that — she deserved a greater place in his heart. Maurice opened his eyes, bewildered. Louis put out his hand and placed it on the boy's thigh as if to say: "Don't worry, I understand these things."

But the boy pushed his hand away roughly. He then made a gesture so unbelievably obscene that it left Bapaume speechless, incapable of saying a word. The sleigh moved away. Over his shoulder, Maurice von Croft shouted: "You don't even understand the trick we played on you! Everybody was in on it! Even my old man! The one with the beauty spot over her mouth isn't Julia, it's Geneviève!" And with his lips curled back like a donkey's, he spattered the countryside with a vulgar bleating that was indisputably the laugh of a perfect idiot.

THE PRISM

HURTUBISE SIGHED WITH RELIEF at the sight of Bapaume's stocky silhouette. The train had left fifteen minutes earlier. The officer had decided to set out on foot to meet the traveller. He asked him why it was that the von Croft boy had not, as agreed, brought him to the station. Louis explained that it was he who had decided to walk the rest of the way. He apologized for having made the lieutenant wait.

"Here's some hot coffee," said Hurtubise once they were seated in front of the fireplace. "When Chouinard comes back I'll ask him to get the bedroom ready for you. The next train isn't till noon tomorrow."

Bapaume replied that it was out of the question; he wanted to leave that evening. He asked how far it was to the next village to the south.

"Why it's more than a three-hour walk, Monsieur Bapaume!"

"There must be some place where I can spend the night. On a train, perhaps? I've caused you enough trouble already . . ."

There were negotiations. Since Bapaume insisted on getting to the next village, the officer finally suggested that he take the freight train that left for Montreal around 2:00 AM. It wouldn't be very comfortable but he'd certainly find some straw to make a bed. The lieutenant knew the stationmaster very well; he'd work something out. He'd write him a note.

"But I still think it's unwise. I imagine your day has been trying enough as it is. You really should accept my invitation. I assure you, it's no trouble."

Bapaume refused to relent.

"As you wish then," said Hurtubise, somewhat shaken by the firmness of which he hadn't thought the traveller capable. He went to his counter to write a brief note to the stationmaster at Saint-G——. "Here, I've given you my address as well. My mother's, actually, but it doesn't matter, it's the same. And you? Could you write yours on this sheet of paper? I haven't given up on my idea of arranging a meeting between your Françoise and mine. Just now, though, you must forgive me; my troop is coming back. I'll be with you in a few minutes."

Hurtubise went out to get news from his men. They had taken part in the unsuccessful mission to rescue the little girl. One member of the team had carried her out of the crevice on his shoulder. They'd come back without attending the religious service. Hurtubise didn't learn anything new. He'd already heard it all on the telephone. The men squeezed together in a row on the front steps, gloomy and despondent. One was sobbing and pulling at his hair. The lieutenant sat down and lit cigarettes of solidarity; they smoked together in silence.

The lieutenant came back inside the building while Bapaume was finishing a letter. He wrote without haste, his pen never leaving the paper, as if the words were coming to him from an unbroken dictation. What a contrast between this self-possession, this confidence, and his dithering the day before! Though the officer prided himself on his knowledge of men, he had to admit that after He'd made this one, God must have broken the mould. With his craggy features, his heavy hands and shoulders, his stocky boar-like appearance, Bapaume resembled a mason who carries a load of bricks on his back. Yet his slightest gesture, even his way of running his hand over his high forehead or of pricking up his ears, of observing you indirectly when your back is turned, of focusing all his attention on the most insignificant objects as if he were probing the depths of their secrets — in all that and beneath his seeming weakness, there was an intriguing and somewhat mysterious subtlety marked by intelligence and simplicity, by the kind of gentleness and strength that are synonymous. And when you least expected it, sometimes this discreet, this reserved, this timid man could give you one of those sharp, devastating looks that strip your heart and soul, that peel away lies and imposture, that leave people exposed like those the lieutenant had seen in the war with their clothes ripped off by a bomb.

Hurtubise sat down beside Bapaume, filled with emotion. He'd have gladly put his arm around his shoulders. "And what about the von Crofts? Were they well?"

"Real live wires," said Bapaume without looking up from his paper. He finished the letter and put it in an envelope. He held it out to the officer. "This is for you."

"For me?"

"I would ask you not to open it till I've gone."

A detail Hurtubise hadn't noticed earlier, now, just as Louis was getting to his feet, chilled his blood. The musician was wearing a belt made from an old length of clothesline. The officer saw that the other man had noticed his shock and he looked away, his face flushed.

"It's about time!" Hurtubise said testily to Chouinard, who was just coming in. "Where have you been all day? I could have used you twenty times."

Chouinard started on some tangled explanations.

"Never mind, we'll discuss that later!"

Bapaume seemed anxious to leave. Hurtubise walked him to the door. He held the traveller's hand in his own for a long moment.

"Your hand is full of music," he said. "It can be felt, I

assure you." The question — "Just between us, tell me, what was your real reason for going there?" — burned his lips. But instead he said: "It's been an honour and a pleasure for me, Monsieur Bapaume. I hope with all my heart that I'll see you again some day."

At first, Bapaume seemed on the verge of saying something. Holding his breath, the officer tried to tell him with his eyes: "You can trust me."

"Something I omitted from my letter. There was a lady in the village . . . she plays the organ in the church . . ."

"Oh yes?" said Hurtubise, waiting for the rest.

But the musician shrugged as if to say, "Why bother?" and doffing his broad-brimmed hat, he stammered a farewell and that was all.

Hurtubise went to the window. Complacently and calmly, the traveller set off along the railway track. "What a peculiar man!" the officer thought to himself. A reliable voice inside him, one that had never lied, told him that this individual was going to become a friend. He opened the envelope. It contained a few dollars.

Saint-Aldor County
23 December 1946

Lieutenant Hurtubise,
My dear friend,
You will find enclosed the money I believe I owe the people at the hotel, which I forgot to give them. I entrust this money to you, certain that it will reach those for whom it is intended. You are an honest man. And I don't believe that one can pay a higher compliment. It's the worst of the sinners who says so.

As for the possibility of a meeting between your Françoise and mine, I must tell you that, alas, such a thing will be impossible. We lost our only son last April and my wife never recovered. She was a person with great virtue in both heart and mind, but she was unable to bear the fact that so essential a piece of our life had collapsed and she has been swallowed up by the avalanche.

Over a period of months I witnessed a terrible thing: the glaciation of a human existence. Françoise was cold, always cold. On the street, in the bright sunshine, in the middle of July. The sight of trees, lawns, flowers made her shudder — the sight of the sky too, because of its emptiness. In the end she shut herself in her room. She would pace up and down all day long, shivering. Can you believe it, Lieutenant? Condensation came from her mouth. During an August heatwave. I tried to reason with her. I know dangerously well how to talk to women, I admit it as a flaw. But with Françoise now, it was a waste of breath. More and more often, for longer and longer periods, she refused to see me. She wrote me letters. Demanding that I go on working, composing the music that would keep her warm. She had become like the living dead, she said and, touching her chest, claimed she could no longer feel her heartbeat. Someone had to find her soul, to catch it as if it were an animal and put it back inside her, restore it to the house of her body. And it was my music that was supposed to set its nets and capture that ailing bird, my oratorio that was supposed to work the miracle. I couldn't do it.

And her ebony hair began to turn white. And I saw ice floes forming around her. The doorknob that I put my hand on every morning was icy. There came a day when I could no longer go inside. The woman I loved was there, on the other side of that door, perishing in an inferno of frost, and there was nothing I could do. No rescue is possible when mountains and rocks and the whole of winter are inside the heart.

And then towards the end, she experienced, I don't know, a kind of appeasement. She started to leave her room again. Sometimes she'd go away and I wouldn't see her for three days. Someone would find her one morning stretched out on a park bench, or walking among hoboes she kept smiling at, very gently, and to whom she'd given away her coats. At this point, she'd say, a thin layer of wool wasn't going to warm her frozen blood . . .

Let me reassure you, Françoise never attempted suicide, nor did she even think that way. But the cold decided for her. No doubt she was braver than I was during the ordeal, in her own way; but, as she was also more pure, she didn't possess the necessary selfishness to choose her own life over the memory she believed she owed her child. It's important to me that you know that. I have written to you because I don't always have the courage to say things out loud. If I'm able to play the organ in the basilica, it's because I am HIDDEN and I feel no one's gaze on me, only that of the Eternal.

My wife had few relatives in Europe and now, because of history, now I fear there is no one left at all. You are the first person with whom I have shared this loss. Should you ever find yourself in possession of a few extra coins, light a candle for the verger's daughter on my behalf.

Farewell and thank you for everything, including having fought in the war.

A. M. G. D.
Louis-Joseph Bapaume

Hurtubise watched the traveller as he moved away. Struck by a sudden thought, Bapaume came to a halt and took something out of his pocket. The distance was too great for Hurtubise to see what it was. The traveller held the object at arm's length so he could gaze at it in the moonlight, the way you look at a photographic negative. Then it fell from his hands and the musician did something so bizarre that, till the end of his life, the officer would wonder if he had seen correctly.

"Lieutenant! Lieutenant!" Chouinard began to shriek as if there were a fire.

Hurtubise ran back to the counter. "What? What is it? What's going on?"

"The teddy bear!" said Chouinard, beside himself. "Where is it? I left it here this morning, on the counter, I'm sure I did!"

"What the hell do I care about your teddy bear!"

Hurtubise returned to the window. He went outside onto the step without bothering to put on a coat. There was nothing to be done. Louis Bapaume had disappeared.

Then, suddenly, what was it? Some vague music coming from somewhere in the mountains. He listened more carefully. No, it must have been just the wind.

Chouinard stood in the middle of the room, arms akimbo. He was bursting with questions.

"What do you think happened to your teddy bear, you imbecile! Are you afraid I stole it? Do you think Monsieur Bapaume took it with him when he left? You prize idiot, you probably lost it yourself!" The officer went upstairs to his room to escape from his own anger and frustration.

The traveller had meticulously folded the blankets and smoothed the sheets and pillow. On the writing desk Hurtubise discovered an illustrated book, *The Nazi Tyranny*, still open. Bapaume must have looked at it. Photos of the death camps. Pensively, the officer turned a few pages. Bits of wood and stones piled into carts, confused piles of mud and garbage where suddenly, mind-bogglingly, you could recognize a shape, a distraught and vacant gaze, teeth and bones, that reminded you that all of it, all the dust and muck, had originally been women, children.

Hurtubise went to the sink to splash water on his face. There was a dead mouse lying above the basin. He picked it up in his handkerchief, grimacing in disgust. He paced for a while. Finally he dropped it into a paper bag the traveller had left behind.

The trap, on the other hand, was nowhere to be found. He got down on all fours to look under the bed and the rest of the furniture. Not that he considered it all that important, but it went against reason and that made him feel uneasy. Near the foot of the writing desk, stuck between two floorboards, was a piece of paper folded in three.

He skimmed the letter, not indiscreetly, simply to see what it was about.

My love, my husband, my great infinite river . . . in the name of our child . . . and I believe that you're embarking on a path that has no meaning but your own destruction . . . should you persist in wanting, on your own, through your own initiative, to hurl yourself into the void . . . come back to your own work too, Louis, to your work! . . . Your wife before God, Françoise.

Hurtubise slipped the paper into his pocket. Bapaume hadn't left his address after all. How would he get this letter to him? The dear man must value it highly to have carried it around with him like that. Perhaps it was the very last letter from his wife. Then the officer realized he could simply send it to Notre-Dame Basilica, "Attention: Substitute Organist."

Through the dormer window he could see the railway track. It occurred to him that the object that had fallen from Bapaume's hands might still be there. The lieutenant went downstairs, grabbed his coat.

He followed the railway track. He had no trouble finding the exact spot. He scanned the landscape: no one, only the motionless countryside, so cold you could hear the nails pop. On the cross-tie, he spied what appeared to be a yellowish pebble at his feet: a tooth. Hurtubise stopped dead. The root was more than half an inch long. What was a tooth doing there? Then, from the snow-covered ballast, he picked up a small glass pyramid. Crouching, the lieutenant studied it: it was a kind of prism. A geometry enthusiast since childhood, he admired its complex structure, which consisted of a multitude of intersecting facets. The lieutenant held it up to the moon, made the light play on it. It was enchanting. Carved letters revealed themselves, depending on the angle from which you observed the prism. The word *real*, the word *disaster*, the word *nothing*. By trial and error, he eventually found the perfect angle of refraction. *No disaster can touch me*, and then, by swivelling the prism slightly, *because nothing is real*. Now he could read a date: *Paris, 8 April 1926*. And these initials: *L. B.* Hurtubise straightened up. The kind of idea you can only have at twenty, he thought, and that life makes sure you'll swallow sooner or later.

The officer tried to mentally reconstruct the scene. He ran his eyes over the footprints from the station to where he was standing now, as if following the walking man. Once again he repeated the traveller's movements, picked up the prism, held it up to the moon and so on, then let it drop into the snow. And that was when the lieutenant was no longer sure of anything. Had the traveller crouched down to look for the prism in the snow? But if so, why had he left it there? Or maybe Hurtubise's eyes were playing tricks on him and the traveller had actually fallen into ecstasy in the middle of the railway tracks — on his knees, arms outstretched, face lifted up to heaven . . .

Hurtubise picked up the glass pyramid. He took the molar and dropped it into his pocket with the prism, as if he dared not separate them, as if nothing can exist on its own. He'd have it all sent to the basilica.

He came back to the station and gazed at the outline of the mountains. The rugged surfaces were iridescent in the last rays of moonlight. He thought this landscape formed a very big mausoleum for a little girl. He preferred to look at the ground as he moved forward. Definitely, the wind was blowing strangely; at times, it seemed you could hear fragments of music.

The lieutenant stopped in the middle of the platform. He opened the letter that the traveller had addressed to him and checked the date of the child's death. Yes, he'd written "last April" . . . twenty years almost to the day that he'd had inscribed on a piece of glass: "No disaster can touch me because nothing is real." Hurtubise sighed.

He was about to put the envelope back in his pocket, already wondering how he'd recount all this to his mother, when a thought came to him. He looked behind him like a man who feels vaguely that he's being followed. But it wasn't that. He was seized by one of the sudden headaches to which he had been subject when he was young, when he thought about matters such as where the universe ended or the loneliness of God before Creation. He took out the letter signed "Françoise" and, holding it in the lamplight, put it next to Bapaume's.

There was no possible doubt: both were written by the same hand.

Longueuil
4 November 1996 – 10 February 1997